The Abbey Mysteries
The Drowned Sword

Other books in the series

The Abbey Mysteries

The Drowned Sword

Cherith Baldry

OXFORD
UNIVERSITY PRESS

OXFORD
UNIVERSITY PRESS

Great Clarendon Street, Oxford OX2 6DP

Oxford University Press is a department of the University of Oxford.
It furthers the University's objective of excellence in research,
scholarship, and education by publishing worldwide in

Oxford New York

Auckland Cape Town Dar es Salaam Hong Kong Karachi
Kuala Lumpur Madrid Melbourne Mexico City Nairobi
New Delhi Shanghai Taipei Toronto

With offices in

Argentina Austria Brazil Chile Czech Republic France Greece
Guatemala Hungary Italy Japan South Korea Poland Portugal
Singapore Switzerland Thailand Turkey Ukraine Vietnam

Oxford is a registered trade mark of Oxford University Press
in the UK and in certain other countries

British Library Cataloguing in Publication Data available

ISBN 0 19 275365 7

1 3 5 7 9 10 8 6 4 2

Printed in Great Britain by
Cox & Wyman Ltd, Reading, Berkshire

Cast of Characters

In the village:

Geoffrey Mason, innkeeper of the Crown in Glastonbury

Idony, his wife

Gwyneth, their daughter

Hereward, their son

Owen Mason, Geoffrey's brother, a stonemason at work on the abbey

Anne Mason, his wife

Matt Green, a stonemason

Clem Ludel, a stonemason

Finn Thorson, the local sheriff

Ivo and Amabel, his twin children, friends of Gwyneth and Hereward

Rhys Freeman, the local shopkeeper

John Brockfield, a farmer

Bryan, the ferryman

Tom Smith, the local smith

Hywel, his brother

Dickon Carver, the local carpenter

Margery Carver, his wife
Mistress Flax, a weaver
Wat and Hankin, brothers, servants at the Crown

At the Abbey:
Henry de Sully, abbot of Glastonbury Abbey
Brother Barnabas, the abbey steward
Brother Padraig, the abbey infirmarian
Brother Timothy, a young monk

Visitors to Glastonbury:
Godfrey de Massard, a priest from Wells Cathedral
Marion le Fevre, an embroideress, come to work
  on the abbey's vestments
Galfridas Hood, her servant
Ursus, a hermit living on Glastonbury Tor
Osbert Teller, a dwarf

Glastonbury, south-west England,
AD 1190

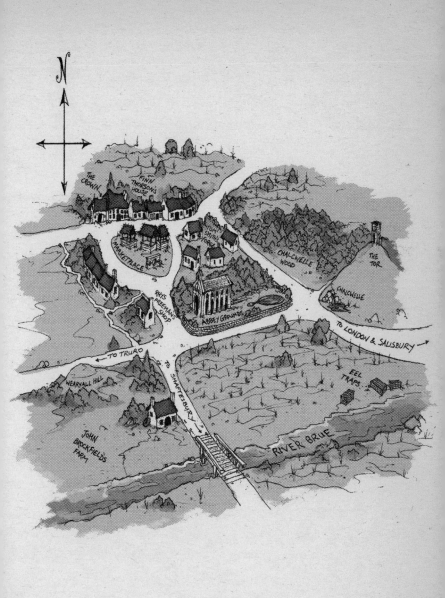

Chapter One

'Master Thorson—wait!' Gwyneth Mason picked up her skirt and hurried after the sheriff of Glastonbury as he propelled her brother Hereward through the door of his house. 'Please listen!'

Finn Thorson didn't stop but disappeared inside, gripping Hereward tightly by one arm and leading his son, Ivo, by the ear. Gwyneth exchanged a despairing glance with her friend Amabel Thorson as the girls followed their brothers inside. In all her years of seeing Finn Thorson deal with villains and scoundrels, Gwyneth had hardly ever seen him so angry.

The sheriff thrust the two boys into the large room where he questioned prisoners. Gwyneth and Amabel stayed in the doorway, anxious to hear what would happen. Rhys Freeman, the shopkeeper, and a local farmer named John

Brockfield were already there, sitting on a bench beside a rough-hewn oak table.

There was an unpleasant look of triumph on Master Freeman's pock-marked face. 'Young limbs of Satan!' he exclaimed when he saw Ivo and Hereward. 'What about your tricks now, hey? You'll be punished, I don't doubt.'

'All in good time, Master Freeman,' Finn Thorson said calmly.

He released the boys and went to sit behind the table, ducking his head of wild red hair to avoid a low beam. His eyes when he looked at Hereward and Ivo were stern; Gwyneth realized that part of the sheriff's anger was because his own son had given Rhys Freeman cause for complaint.

'Well?' the sheriff demanded. 'What have you to say for yourselves?'

'It was only a jest, father,' said Ivo. 'We never meant—'

'Never meant!' Master Freeman interrupted loudly. 'You've been naught but trouble since the day you were born—you and that sister of yours.'

'That's not fair!' Amabel protested. 'It wasn't me took the pig.'

4

'But you were in my shop, weren't you?' Rhys Freeman swung round and glared at her. 'Accusing me of watering my wine! And the shop full of pilgrims—rich pilgrims, too, with money in their purses.' His face took on an injured look. 'I don't know how an honest man's supposed to make a living here,' he whined.

'Less of the "honest man", Rhys,' said Finn Thorson. Gwyneth guessed he was thinking of the time when the shopkeeper had traded in fake holy relics, and had stolen the newly discovered bones of King Arthur from the abbey. She and Hereward had helped to find them again, and Master Freeman had never forgiven them for the spell he had spent in the stocks.

'Let's concentrate on what happened today, shall we?' the sheriff continued, his expression as cold as the December day outside. 'Ivo, start from the beginning. What were you and Amabel doing in Master Freeman's shop?'

'We went with Gwyneth and Hereward,' Ivo said.

'Mother sent us to buy lamp oil,' Hereward added virtuously. He was trying to look earnest and responsible, but the effect was somewhat spoilt by the streaks of mud down his face and his tunic, and his wildly dishevelled chestnut hair.

'And that took four of you, did it?' the sheriff queried, raising his eyebrows. 'Very well; go on.'

'There were pilgrims to the abbey there, buying wine.' Gwyneth was glad that it was Hereward who had taken it on himself to explain; he was more likely to tell the story sensibly than Ivo, who always spoke first and thought afterwards. 'And . . . and Ivo said that the last lot of wine from Master Freeman's shop had been watered.'

'But it had!' Ivo exclaimed hotly.

'And you shouted it out so all the village could hear you,' Rhys Freeman complained—making no attempt to gainsay the charge, Gwyneth noticed.

The sheriff looked down at his hands. Gwyneth knew very well the accusation that Rhys Freeman put water in his wine was true. Her mother and father, who owned the Crown Inn, had stopped buying wine from him long ago, sure that it wouldn't be fit for their guests to drink. Now that lots of pilgrims were visiting the village to see King Arthur's bones, not to mention travellers coming to gawp at Chalcwelle where a man had been found murdered, it was more important than ever to have good food and wine to offer them.

'What happened after you made your accusations, Ivo?' Finn Thorson prompted.

'Master Freeman threw us out,' Ivo replied indignantly. 'He kicked us!' He glared at the shopkeeper and rubbed his behind.

'And mother still hasn't got her lamp oil,' Hereward put in.

Finn Thorson took a deep breath and let it out again. 'So you insulted Master Freeman and he threw you out of his shop. And there the matter might have ended. But no—you had to go and steal a pig.'

'We didn't steal it!' Ivo's freckled face flushed with anger. 'We borrowed it.'

'Borrowed it,' his father echoed. He clasped his hands together so tightly that the knuckles turned white. 'Master Brockfield, did you agree to lend these boys a pig?'

John Brockfield shook his head. He was a short, stocky man with thinning grey hair and a weathered, wrinkled face. Gwyneth suspected that he was trying to hide a smile, for his eyes were twinkling, though he kept them fixed firmly on the sheriff. 'Nay, Master Thorson, they didn't ask. But the pig has taken no hurt, and I have it back safely.'

'That's not the point,' the sheriff said curtly. 'Hereward, tell me what happened then.'

Hereward shuffled his feet and cast an uneasy look over his shoulder at Gwyneth. 'I took an onion from mother's storeroom,' he confessed. 'Ivo and I used it to lure the pig away from Master Brockfield's pen in the market-place.' His voice trailed off.

'And then?'

'We threw the onion into Master Freeman's shop.' Ivo took up the story, unable to hide a note of pride in his voice. 'The pig ran in after it.'

'Frightening my customers into fits!' Rhys Freeman exclaimed. 'And it broke a stack of jugs. I'll expect compensation for them.'

'You'll get all you're entitled to, Rhys.' Finn Thorson's voice was clipped. 'And then you girls chased the pig . . . ?'

'We went in after it,' Gwyneth admitted.

'We *caught* it,' Amabel corrected her. With a

furious glance at her brother she went on, '*They* were laughing like lunatics. I might have known they would get us into trouble.'

'The young wenches brought the pig back,' John Brockfield said mildly. 'I reckon they weren't part of the mischief.'

'Mischief, you call it!' Rhys Freeman snorted. 'It's wickedness, that's what it is, and all four of them were in it together.' He gleefully rubbed his hands together. 'Well, you'll get what's coming to you now.'

Finn Thorson paused for a moment, looking into the faces of the four who were accused. Gwyneth burned with humiliation as his eyes fell on her and she saw disappointment in his cold blue stare. She hadn't taken any part in the trick with the pig—though it had been funny to see it dashing to and fro in Rhys Freeman's shop, with Mistress Flax shrieking as she tried to get out of its way and Master Freeman swiping at it with a broom in the midst of shattering crockery. But it was not so funny now, to be blamed with the boys for what had happened.

The sheriff set his hands flat on the table and

levered himself to his feet, looking down on the boys from his great height.

'First, the compensation.' His voice was firm but expressionless. 'Geoffrey Mason and I will divide the cost of the broken jugs between us, and pay Master Freeman for his loss.'

'So I should hope,' puffed the shopkeeper, smoothing his tunic over his paunch. 'Fine pottery, that was.'

'I shall ask Brother Barnabas the abbey steward to assess the value,' the sheriff went on. 'Will that be agreeable to you. Rhys?'

Rather sulkily, Master Freeman agreed. Gwyneth guessed that left to himself he would have put a much higher value on the jugs than they were really worth.

'As to punishment . . .' Finn Thorson's gaze swept over the four friends again. 'Ivo and Amabel, you will go with Master Freeman to clear up his shop. When I come to check, I want to be able to eat my dinner off the floor.'

'But that's not fair!' Ivo stared at his father in horror. 'That place is filthy! He'll have us clearing up all the dirt from the last six months.'

'Then perhaps you'll remember that next time

10

you plan a trick,' Finn Thorson said unsympathetically. 'Go on, Master Freeman, they're yours for the rest of the day.'

Smiling broadly, Rhys Freeman grabbed Ivo by the shoulder and thrust him towards the door. Ivo shook him off with a furious look and stalked out. Amabel stood her ground and muttered mutinously, 'It wasn't *my* fault. I don't see why I—'

'Do as you're bid,' her father ordered; he sounded so angry that Amabel's eyes widened and she scuttled out after her brother.

Rhys Freeman followed, pausing in the doorway to remark, 'You're a fair man, Master Thorson, I'll say that for you.'

Finn Thorson said no more until the sound of their footsteps died away; Gwyneth heard the door to the street open and close with a brief flash of noise from the busy market-place outside. Her stomach churned as she wondered what punishment the sheriff had in mind for her and Hereward.

'Now, young Hereward,' he began.

The sound of galloping hooves in the street interrupted him, followed by a loud hammering on the outer door. Gwyneth heard one of Master Thorson's men opening the door, and heavy footsteps tramped down the passage.

A tall hooded man entered the room with a swirl of his black cloak and halted in front of the sheriff. 'Finn Thorson?' he demanded, looking from Finn to John Brockfield.

The sheriff stepped forward. 'I am. And you, sir?'

The newcomer pushed back his hood to reveal a thin, bearded face above a gleaming shirt of chain mail. 'I am the under-sheriff of Bristol,' he announced, 'and I come with grave news. Yesterday a band of traitors escaped just as they were about to be hanged for their crimes. It's thought they might have come this way.'

Traitors! Gwyneth glanced excitedly at Hereward, whose eyebrows had nearly vanished into his hair.

'There's a letter from the sheriff will tell you more,' the stranger went on, pulling a folded parchment from his cloak and tossing it down on the table.

'One moment,' said Finn Thorson. 'Hereward and Gwyneth, go with Master Brockfield. You're to clean out the pig shelter in the field over the river. Master Brockfield, make sure they do it well.'

'I will that,' John Brockfield replied, with a wink at Hereward. 'Yon shelter's not been touched for a seven-night.'

He shepherded them out through the door. Gwyneth glanced back as she followed her brother into the passage, to see Finn Thorson break the seal of the letter and unfold the crackling parchment. He began to read quietly under his breath as Master Brockfield closed the door, and Gwyneth could hear no more.

Gwyneth sat glumly on a log near John Brockfield's pig shelter, a spade lying at her feet. Grey clouds hung low and threatening in the sky, and there was a sting of sleet in the wind. The hollow of an old lake-bed stretched in front of her, with a muddy pool at its centre where three or four of Master Brockfield's pigs were wallowing contentedly. Beyond, a line of reeds and leafless willow trees marked the course of the river.

Huddling deeper into her cloak for warmth, Gwyneth thought crossly that this was the last place she would choose to be on a raw December afternoon. Back home at the Crown, the kitchen would be filled with delicious spicy smells as her mother baked Yuletide treats for the feast that was only a few days away. Instead of helping her, Gwyneth was stuck in this cold, muddy field where the only way to keep warm was to help Hereward with digging out the pig shelter; but she would rather die than share the punishment that she had never deserved.

Her thoughts soon strayed to the arrival of the under-sheriff of Bristol, and the news he had brought. A band of escaped traitors, perhaps making for the Glastonbury area . . . Gwyneth shivered, half expecting to see desperate men galloping along the track from the ferry at that very moment, brandishing their swords.

'Hey!' Hereward's voice, loud with indignation, interrupted her thoughts. Gwyneth turned to see him standing in the doorway of the wood-walled hut, a spade in his hand and his chest-nut hair plastered to his forehead with sweat.

'Aren't you coming to help?' he demanded. 'Master Thorson sent both of us to do this.'

'*I* didn't steal a pig,' Gwyneth pointed out. 'I don't see why I should have to clean out their filthy shelter.'

'You thought it was funny as much as we did,' Hereward protested, driving the spade into the ground and walking out of the hut. 'You were as glad as anybody to see that pig in Master Freeman's shop.'

'And a lot of good it did you! Now we're stuck out here in the freezing cold. I could have been helping mother with her baking, or Mistress le Fevre with her embroidery.'

'Mistress le Fevre and her precious embroidery . . . that's all we ever hear from you.' Hereward had gone red with anger. 'Are you going to help or not?'

'No.' Gwyneth pressed her lips together determinedly.

Hereward bent down, scooped up a handful of mud, and flung it at Gwyneth. 'Then take that!' he yelled.

She sprang up and tried to dodge out of the way, but too late. The clod hit the ground close to her feet and splattered upwards, over her cloak and the front of her gown.

'Now look what you've done!' Furious, Gwyneth ran at her brother and shoved him with both hands.

Hereward staggered backwards, lost his footing, and slid down into the lake-bed, rolling over until something brought him to an abrupt stop just short of the muddy pool. Master Brockfield's pigs raised their snouts and gave him a curious look from small, bright eyes.

Spitting out mud, Hereward hauled himself to his hands and knees. Slimy brownish-green mud plastered his face and the front of his tunic. Gwyneth couldn't resist bursting into laughter at the sight of him.

'It's not funny!' Hereward shouted. 'I've hit my head on something.'

Gwyneth stopped laughing at once; she hadn't meant Hereward to be hurt. 'Was it a stone? Is your head bleeding?' she asked anxiously, coming to stand at the edge of the hollow.

Hereward rubbed his head, smearing more wet earth into his hair. 'No, a root, I think. It was sharp, though.' He groped in the mud in front of him and grasped something with one hand. His expression grew puzzled. 'No, it's not a root, it's . . .' His voice trailed off, and when he spoke again he sounded astonished.

'Gwyneth, look at this!'

Chapter Two

'What is it?' asked Gwyneth.

Instead of answering, Hereward scrambled to his feet and tugged with both hands, drawing something long and slender out of the mud. He was just turning towards Gwyneth when she spotted a dark shape on the path that led to the ferry. The River Brue divided John Brockfield's land in two, and to reach his pigs he had to cross by the bridge close to his farm, or further upstream by using the flat-bottomed boat that Bryan the ferryman poled to and fro.

'Hereward!' Gwyneth called. 'Master Brockfield is coming back.'

At once Hereward dropped the object so that the water at the edge of the pool closed over it. He stared down at it as if he wanted to make sure it was concealed before floundering up the slope to where Gwyneth was standing.

'What are you doing?' she whispered. 'What was that in the mud?'

Hereward shook his head. 'I'll tell you later.'

John Brockfield trudged towards them, his shoulders bent under a yoke with a heavy wooden bucket at either end. A broad grin spread over the farmer's face when he saw Hereward. 'Well, lad, you were supposed to clean the shelter, but there was no call to spread the muck all over yourself.'

Hereward shrugged, looking embarrassed.

'How goes the work?' the farmer continued. 'Have you finished yet?'

'No.' Hereward shot a resentful look at Gwyneth. 'Not quite.'

John Brockfield smiled, taking the sting out of his words as he said, 'Then put your backs into it. 'Twill be dark soon.' His eyes twinkled kindly as he added, 'And if you stop by the cottage on your way home, perhaps Mistress Brockfield will have a pasty ready for you.'

Hereward brightened. 'Thank you, Master Brockfield!' Hurriedly he retrieved his spade and headed back into the pig shelter.

John Brockfield took each of the wooden

19

buckets in turn, and tipped a sloppy stream of pig mash into a stone trough outside the shelter. The pigs in the pool heaved themselves out of the mud, trotted up the slope and buried their snouts in the steaming mash.

The farmer watched them with a contented smile as they snorted and nudged each other for the best positions. Then he nodded farewell to Gwyneth and turned back towards the ferry. Gwyneth watched him out of sight, before resignedly picking up the second spade and following her brother into the shelter.

The sun was going down by the time they had finished their task.

'There!' said Gwyneth, picking up a handful of straw to clean her spade. 'That's done.'

'It's a palace for pigs now,' Hereward remarked, surveying the clean floor covered with a layer of fresh straw. He had recovered from his ill-temper as soon as Gwyneth had come to share the work with him.

'It won't be for long, though.' Gwyneth pushed stray wisps of hair away from her face with a muddy hand. 'They'll make it just as dirty.'

'That's pigs for you,' Hereward said with a grin. Leaving his spade leaning against the wall of the shelter he walked out of the hut and headed straight for the lake-bed.

Gwyneth stood in the doorway and stared after him. 'What are you doing? If you don't come now, we won't be home before dark.'

Hereward did not reply. He stooped over the pool and fished around under the water until he came up with the stick-like object he had pulled out earlier. Clutching it in both hands, he struggled back up the slope to where Gwyneth was standing.

'What is it?' she asked, thoroughly curious by now. 'Let me see.'

She reached out a hand but, instead of giving the object to her, Hereward took a step back, a defensive look in his eyes. After a brief pause he held it out so she could look at it, but his fingers stayed firmly wrapped around the thicker end.

It was a sword. The blade was longer than Gwyneth's arm, narrow and tapering, and the hilt was thick and heavy. It looked old; both the hilt and the blade were covered in rust.

'What a strange thing to find!' Gwyneth exclaimed. 'A knight must have dropped it there long ago. Or maybe he fell in, when there was a lake here . . .' She broke off with a shiver, imagining the drowned warrior lying undiscovered for many, many years; perhaps his bones still rested beneath the waters of the pool!

As if he had not heard her, Hereward swished the sword through the air. 'I'd like to be a knight,' he murmured.

He held the sword close to his face to examine it again. Gwyneth thought she could make out a pattern on the hilt that looked vaguely familiar—the shape of some coiled creature wreathed in thorns—but when she bent over to see better Hereward pulled the sword away.

'Let's get home,' he said abruptly. He laid the sword aside, but only to pick up his cloak. Then he grasped the sword again and headed down the track that led to the ferry.

'Hereward, wait!' Gwyneth grabbed both spades and hurried after her brother. 'What are you doing? Are you going to take that sword to Master Brockfield?'

Hereward halted and turned his head to stare

at her. There was a strange light in his eyes that unnerved Gwyneth, until she realized that it must be the reflection of the setting sun.

'No,' he said. 'It's mine. I found it.' He swung the sword upwards as he spoke, his grimy fingers curled tightly around the hilt.

Gwyneth took a step back to dodge the hissing blade. 'Be careful!' Shrugging, she added, 'Well, keep it if you want. I don't suppose Master Brockfield has any use for a rusty old thing like that.'

Hereward did not say another word until they came to the ferry and were waiting for the ferryman to punt his flat-bottomed boat over from the other side of the river. Holding the sword close to his body, Hereward pulled a fold of his cloak over it to hide it. 'Don't tell Bryan about it,' he muttered. 'You know once he knows, so will the whole village, and half of Wells, too.'

Gwyneth wondered whether her brother was feeling guilty, as if he was stealing the sword. 'There's no need to be so secretive,' she said. 'No one will mind. It's just an old sword.'

Hereward frowned. 'It might not be so old,'

23

he said. 'How do we know where it came from? Just don't mention it.'

Before Gwyneth could reply, Bryan was hailing them, and a moment later the prow of his boat nudged into the bank so that they could step on board.

'Good evening, Bryan,' Gwyneth greeted him. 'Can you take us across?'

Bryan smiled down at her. He was a tall, gangling man, with the lanky limbs of a heron, and long mouse-coloured hair which he wore tied back with a scrap of twine.

'Good evening, Gwyneth and Hereward,' he said. 'Step aboard. Master Brockfield told me to expect you. You've heard the news?' he added as he held out a hand to Gwyneth to steady her. 'About the traitors that escaped from hanging in Bristol?'

Gwyneth nodded excitedly. Hereward was right—Bryan was a great gossip, and he would be sure to have the latest news. He lived alone like the hermits on the Tor, but unlike them he was always ready to talk.

As he pushed the boat away from the bank, the ferryman went on, 'I had one of Finn

Thorson's men in my boat. He told me all about it. Over in Bristol, they think the traitors were Henry of Truro's men.'

'Henry of Truro!' Gwyneth echoed. She glanced at Hereward, but her brother was hunched at the front of the boat with one hand resting protectively on the fold in his cloak that hid the sword.

She and Hereward had heard of Henry many times before; he was King Richard's cousin, and had already made one attempt to assassinate the king and seize the throne for himself. Richard had sent Henry into exile in Wales, but rumours had reached Glastonbury that the traitor was gathering men for another attempt on the throne while his cousin was away in the Holy Land.

'Did Henry send his men to free the traitors?' Gwyneth asked.

'I don't rightly know.' Bryan dug his pole into the river bed and sent the boat gliding across the river. 'Finn Thorson's man said horsemen galloped into the square just when the men were being led out to be hanged. They fired blazing arrows into the crowd, and everybody panicked.'

'That's terrible!' gasped Gwyneth, shivering as

she thought of flames leaping up, men and women screaming and trying to escape, trampling hooves . . . 'Were many people hurt?'

'Not many, from what I hear,' replied Bryan. 'No thanks to Henry's men, mind you. They're desperate souls, and no mistaking. They rode straight through the crowd to cut the prisoners free, pulled them up on their horses and fled as fast as they could.' He paused and added dramatically, 'There's some as say they flew out of the square.'

'Oh, don't be ridiculous,' Hereward snapped, without turning to look at Bryan. 'Nobody can fly.'

Bryan laughed, quite unoffended by Hereward's ill-tempered remark. 'No more they can. But those villains got clean away, just as if they could. Their tracks led in this direction, but by the time the sheriff of Bristol sent his men after them, they were long gone.'

He guided the boat neatly up against the far bank of the river and looped the mooring-rope around a stake. 'There you are, young master and mistress. And don't worry none about a coin for your passage. Master Brockfield saw to all that.'

Gwyneth thanked him and jumped onto the bank, hurrying after Hereward, who had stalked off without a word.

'Get you home now!' Bryan called after them. 'There might be evil men about.'

'We will!' Gwyneth turned to wave, hot with shame that her brother was being so rude. 'You could have thanked Bryan,' she puffed, running to catch Hereward up. 'You never even said goodbye.'

'What?' Hereward's gaze seemed to focus on something she couldn't see. 'Come on, it's getting late.'

'We've got to take the spades back,' Gwyneth pointed out. 'And don't forget Mistress Brockfield's pasties.'

Hereward gave her a puzzled look as if he had no idea what she was talking about. Gwyneth suddenly felt wary. There must be something wrong with her brother if he could forget so completely about food. But he had changed direction so that his footsteps were taking him towards John Brockfield's squat stone farm-house; Gwyneth shrugged and hurried after him, guessing that Hereward was distracted by news of the escaped traitors, and the possibility that the fugitives might be heading for their very own village.

Hereward strode along the muddy track that led from John Brockfield's cottage to the village. In one hand he held one of Mistress Brockfield's pasties, half-eaten and stuffed with pork and beans, and in the other he held the sword. It rested lightly in his fingers, perfectly balanced between blade and hilt. Slicing it through the air, Hereward dreamed that one day he might be a knight, and carry a sword exactly like this in the defence of his king.

I'd use it now if I could, he thought loyally. *Just let Henry of Truro show his face. Then he'd see.*

Gwyneth would see, too, he added to himself, swallowing the last of his pasty and rubbing his fingers on his tunic. He was fond of his sister, but she fussed too much. Just because she was a year older she treated him as if he was still a little boy, even though he was twelve years old, almost a man. She was somewhere ahead of him now, in the woods that grew between the village and the river, calling to him to hurry so that they could get back to the inn before it was dark. As if there was any danger, while he had the sword! The weapon sent warmth through his fingers into his whole body, making him feel tall and tireless, ready to meet any threats that might be lurking among the dark trees.

A tangle of hawthorn branches overhung the path, outlined against the twilight sky. Without stopping to wonder if a rusty blade that had been buried for Lord knows how long would be able to cut through anything, Hereward raised the sword and slashed it through them; the tough stems parted as easily as if he had drawn a hot knife through butter.

There was a quiet chuckle from behind him.

'Collecting firewood, young Hereward?' said a familiar voice.

Without thinking, Hereward opened his fingers and dropped the sword in the long grass beside the path. Whirling round and peering through the dusk, he said, 'Ursus, is that you?'

'It is.' Ursus stepped out of the shadows, then bent down to gather up the branches and presented them to Hereward. He clutched them to his chest, hoping that the hermit would not ask him how he had cut them with no sign of an axe about him. Both he and Gwyneth liked and trusted Ursus, who lived in a cell somewhere on the slopes of Glastonbury Tor. They had shared many adventures with him, but every time he helped them to discover something new, they realized how little they knew about their friend. And right now, something whispered inside Hereward's head that he should not share the discovery of the drowned sword with the hermit—at least, not yet.

'Is your sister not with you?' Ursus asked.

'Yes, I'm here.' Gwyneth appeared from further up the path. 'Well met, Ursus.'

Ursus bowed. 'And I am glad to see you, as always. But I did not expect to see you so far from the village this late.'

Hereward felt himself flushing with guilt, and was relieved that the gathering darkness would hide his reddened cheeks. Was it possible that Ursus had seen him drop the sword into the grass? But the hermit said nothing more.

There's no need to feel guilty, Hereward told himself stoutly. *I haven't done anything wrong.*

'Have you heard the latest news about Henry of Truro?' asked Gwyneth. 'Some of his men have escaped from Bristol jail.'

'I had not heard,' Ursus said gravely. 'This is ill news.'

'They might have come this way,' Hereward put in. 'Finn Thorson has been told to look out for them.'

'I'm sure that if any man can trap them, Master Thorson can,' said Ursus. 'But meanwhile I will not keep you here. You must not wander the woods at night.' He raised one hand in farewell and melted into the darkness under the trees.

As soon as Hereward was sure he had gone, he dropped the hawthorn branches and scrabbled in the long grass until his hand closed once more over the hilt of the sword. Once again it seemed to tingle in his grip, warming him from head to toe, and he was filled with blazing certainty that if Henry of Truro and his whole army leapt out to face them at that very moment, he would be able to vanquish them all.

Chapter Three

As soon as Gwyneth had washed and changed out of her mud-spattered gown, she hurried into the kitchen where her mother was preparing the evening meal for their guests.

'There you are!' Idony Mason exclaimed, sounding harassed as she piled loaves into a large basket. 'I've had to do without you all day, thanks to that runaway pig.'

'It wasn't my fault.' Gwyneth protested her innocence for what felt like the thousandth time. 'It was Ivo and Hereward.'

'But you and Amabel weren't far behind, I'll warrant,' said Idony. 'And now we have to pay Master Freeman half the cost of his jugs. As if we hadn't two places to put every penny as it is! All the same, I wish I'd seen the pig in his shop,' she confessed. Her mouth twitched, and Gwyneth thought she was trying not to laugh.

32

She added one last loaf to the basket and pushed it across the table. 'There, take those into the taproom to your father,' said Idony. 'Where's Hereward?'

'He went to the stables,' Gwyneth replied. Hereward had muttered something about putting the sword away when they finally reached the inn yard.

'Well, if you see him send him in here,' her mother said, whisking across the kitchen to the fire and stirring the pot of soup that bubbled there. 'I could do with another pair of hands.'

Gwyneth picked up the basket and used one foot to open the door to the taproom. The air was warm with the scent of honey and ale that Geoffrey Mason mixed to fill the huge wassail bowl over the Christmas season. A wave of talk and laughter came out to greet Gwyneth, suddenly interrupted by the sound of a fist thumped down on a table and one voice raised above the rest.

'And I tell you Richard is no true king!'

Gwyneth was so shocked that she almost dropped the basket. The speaker was Clem Ludel, one of the stonemasons who were building the new church for Glastonbury Abbey. He was a short, burly man with a thatch of straw-coloured hair, and right now his face was so deeply flushed that Gwyneth guessed he had been dipping his mug too often in the wassail bowl.

'What should a king do for us?' Master Ludel climbed up on a bench to make himself better heard, and stood there swaying unsteadily with his pot of ale in his hand. 'Should he not stay here and make good laws, and . . . and guard his people from thieves and raiders? Does Richard do this? No, I tell you he does not! He leaves us all to go traipsing off to foreign parts!'

A babble of voices was raised in protest. Gwyneth saw her uncle, Owen Mason, tug at Master Ludel's arm to fetch him down from the bench, but Ludel shook him off. Taking another long draught of his ale, he shouted, 'Richard has left us—and that makes him no king of ours!'

The clamour grew louder. One man jumped to his feet, and someone else yelled, 'Treason!' An empty pot flew through the air and struck Master Ludel full in the chest. He stumbled backwards off the bench and landed with a thud against the wall, ale slopping down the front of his tunic. Dickon Carver, the carpenter, grabbed him by the collar, his fist raised.

Gwyneth looked around helplessly for her father, and was relieved to see Geoffrey Mason thrusting his way through the crowd. Reaching Master Carver, he rested one hand on his shoulder and said something rapidly to him that Gwyneth could not hear. Master Carver released Ludel with a grim nod and Geoffrey Mason took his place, grasping the drunken stonemason by the arm and propelling him towards the outer door.

'We'll have none of that talk here, Master Ludel,' he said firmly. 'Do you want us all hanged for treason?'

Gwyneth held the door wide open for her father, catching the reek of ale from Master Ludel's breath as he was shoved past her. The two men crashed out into the inn yard, Ludel still protesting loudly.

The uproar in the taproom was already beginning to quieten down. Uncle Owen shook his head and remarked to no one in particular. 'When the ale is in, the wit is out. But Clem Ludel was ever a hothead.'

Sighing with relief, Gwyneth began to distribute the bread. She noticed a cloaked stranger seated at a table in one corner with a pot of ale in front of him. She went over to him and bobbed a curtsy. 'Bread, sir?'

The man looked up. He had a pale, hard face, with reddish hair cropped close to his head. Most startling of all, his eyes were mismatched, one blue and one brown. Gwyneth knew that she had seen him before, but at first she could not recall where. As she set a loaf down on the table and turned away, she remembered that he was the servant of Marion le Fevre, the embroideress who was living at the Crown while she worked on new altar cloths and vestments for the abbey. He had escorted Mistress le Fevre when she had first arrived, but stayed no more than a day or two. He must have returned on an errand from the embroideress's home in Wales, Gwyneth guessed, and she hoped the man would not think she was rude because she could not remember his name.

The man and his mismatched eyes slipped out of her mind as Uncle Owen beckoned her over for his share of the bread, and the cheerful bubble of conversation rose up around her once again. Traitors or no, the Crown was as busy as ever with local folk and pilgrims, all wanting the finest ale and food that Glastonbury could provide.

Hereward finally made his escape from Wat, who had kept him in the stable to help him fill the mangers with hay as soon as he spotted Hereward coming into the inn yard. Dodging quickly through the door, he wrapped the sword in a piece of sacking he had taken from the place where Wat stored feed for the guests' horses. As he gazed around, wondering where would be a good place to hide it, the door from the taproom crashed open and lamplight flooded into the yard. Hereward's father appeared, pushing one of the stonemasons in front of him.

Hereward recognized Clem Ludel from his fair hair and sturdy frame; he was shouting incoherently and struggling to free himself, but Geoffrey Mason's grip was firm. He thrust Master Ludel across the yard as far as the well and forced him to his knees. Reaching for the bucket that hung from the well-head, he upended it and doused Master Ludel's head in a cascade of water. Ludel yelled, and Hereward winced in sympathy, knowing how icy the water would be at this time of year.

'Clear your head, Master Ludel,' Geoffrey Mason ordered. 'When you're sober you'll be welcome inside, but not before.'

He turned and went back into the taproom. Ludel, still crouched beside the well, shouted a curse after him. Geoffrey Mason ignored him and closed the door, leaving the yard in darkness, with no other sound than the mutterings of the drenched stonemason.

Hereward was preparing to slip past into the inn when quick footsteps sounded from the street, and a tall, broad-shouldered man strode under the archway. There was just enough light for Hereward to recognize Matt Green, another of the stonemasons.

Spotting Clem Ludel, he walked over to the well and stood looking down with his arms folded and a grin on his face.

'Taking a bath, Clem?' he asked. 'Bad for the health, that is.'

Master Ludel looked up, blinking through the water that dripped from his hair, and spat out something Hereward could not hear.

'Steady, lad,' said Matt, still grinning. 'There's no call for language like that. Upset Master Mason, did you?'

Clem Ludel scrambled up until he was sitting on the stone coping of the well; Hereward was half prepared for him to topple backwards into the shaft, and hoped that Matt Green would grab him if he started to fall. His tunic was soaked and his fair hair darkened by the water and plastered flat against his head. His face was set in an ugly expression of fury.

'What's the world coming to if a man can't speak his mind?' he complained. 'But he'll see . . . one day soon he'll see . . .'

'What will he see, Clem?'

'Who should be true king of England,' Ludel shot back at him.

Matt Green's grin vanished abruptly. 'That's treasonous talk.'

Ludel shook his head as if to clear it and slicked back his dripping hair. ''S not treason to love your country. 'S not treason to speak the truth. King Richard cares naught for us, and you know that as well as I do.'.

'I know no such thing,' Master Green replied. 'And nor do you, Clem, when the ale's out of you.'

Anger flared up again in Clem Ludel's face. 'I'm not so drunk . . . not so drunk that I don't know . . .'

'What do you know?'

'More than you. More than those fools in there. I know about the Hoodman.'

'The Hoodman? And who's that?' Matt Green let out a short bark of laughter. 'A bugaboo to frighten children with?'

'You're touched in the head if you think that, Matt Green. The Hoodman is Henry of Truro's most trusted man.'

Hereward stiffened and took a step or two forward, keeping to the shadows, so that he would not miss a word of the conversation. Henry of Truro had been mentioned more than once already today, blamed for the escaped prisoners in Bristol, and now Clem Ludel seemed to know even more about him than Bryan the ferryman.

'The Hoodman is raising an army,' Master

Ludel went on. 'He'll fight for Henry and sweep Richard away.' He let out a deep belch. 'And them that fight with him will have wealth and land. I'll be rich, Matt Green, richer than you'll ever be, chipping stone all day. You'd do well to join us.'

Master Green stared at him. 'Man, you're drunk as a drowned mouse,' he said derisively. 'The only reward you'll ever see on that road is a prison cell and a rope. I like my neck as it is, thank you.'

'Then you're a fool!' Clem Ludel lurched to his feet and prodded Master Green in the chest with one finger. 'The Hoodman looks after his own. Who do you think rescued those men from Bristol jail?'

Matt Green gaped in genuine surprise and, in the shadows, so did Hereward. He barely noticed his fingers closing instinctively around the hilt of the sword. 'What do you know about that?' demanded the stonemason.

'More than you. I know 'twas the Hoodman led the men into the square and fired blazing arrows to frighten the crowd and give him the chance to cut the prisoners free.' Master Ludel

41

grabbed Matt's shoulders and shook him. 'Join us, Matt. Henry will reward us when he's king.'

Matt Green pushed Ludel away from him and stepped out of the range of his grasping hands. 'Go home and sleep it off, Clem, and come back when your head's clear.' Turning away, he marched across the yard and went into the taproom.

'Fool!' Clem Ludel called after him. 'You'll see! When Henry's king . . .' His voice trailed away. A moment later he straightened up and stumbled across the cobbles towards the archway.

As he vanished into the street, Hereward let out a long breath. *Who could the Hoodman be?* he wondered. Whoever the mystery man was, he was powerful enough to arrange for the rescue of men on their way to the gallows; what's more, if Clem Ludel could be believed, he was recruiting an army to fight against King Richard and put Henry of Truro on the throne of England. And, most serious of all, the Hoodman—or his men—was looking for supporters in Glastonbury.

Hereward felt his fingers close around the hilt of the sword inside the piece of sacking. He wanted to think that it was all nothing more than the rantings of a drunkard. But he could not convince himself. Clem Ludel had not been so drunk that he was beyond speaking reason— growing up at the Crown, Hereward had seen enough men in their cups who could string barely two words together, let alone a whole sentence. No, the Hoodman was real, and his treason was threatening the peace of the whole country and the reign of their king all over again.

Chapter Four

'Psst—Gwyneth!'

She spun round to see her brother poking his head around the door that led to the inn yard. When Hereward saw that she was alone in the kitchen, he came in and shut the door quietly behind him.

'I need to talk to you,' he said. 'Where's mother?'

'In the scullery,' Gwyneth replied. 'She's been asking where you are.' Looking her brother up and down, she saw that he was still wearing his soiled tunic, and his hands and face were streaked with mud from Master Brockfield's pigs. At least he wasn't lugging that old sword around any longer. 'Mother will be furious if she sees you in the kitchen like that,' she added.

Hereward shook his head irritably. 'That's not important,' he said. 'Something's happened.'

'What?' Gwyneth's curiosity was roused and she paused in chopping onions, setting the knife down on the table. 'I know that Mistress le Fevre's servingman is back. The one with the unmatched eyes, remember? And Clem Ludel got drunk in the taproom—'

'That's it,' Hereward interrupted. 'Clem Ludel. I saw father throw him out, then Matt Green came into the yard. Master Ludel told him about a man called the Hoodman, who's raising an army for Henry of Truro. He set the prisoners free from Bristol. Clem Ludel has joined them, and he was trying to get Matt Green to join too.' He finished in a rush, and stared expectantly at his sister.

Gwyneth's heart started to pound. Could treason have really come to Glastonbury, as Bryan the ferryman had warned? 'But Clem Ludel was drunk,' she pointed out.

'Just because he was drunk doesn't mean it isn't true,' Hereward argued. 'The drink made him talk too much, that's all.'

'What do you think we should do?' Gwyneth fiddled with the knife handle. 'Tell Master Thorson?'

Hereward snorted. 'He'll never believe us, after

the trouble we got into with Master Brockfield's pig.'

Gwyneth sighed in exasperation, but decided that telling Hereward yet again that the business of the pig had been his and Ivo's fault alone was a waste of breath. 'Father Godfrey, then,' she suggested. 'He'll listen to us.'

Godfrey de Massard was a priest from Wells who had been staying at Glastonbury Abbey for some months now. At first Gwyneth and Hereward had suspected him of being a spy for Dean Alexander of Wells, who wanted to bring Glastonbury under his own authority. However, Father Godfrey seemed more interested in tracking down Henry of Truro than in priestly duties. He had been coldly dismissive of Gwyneth and Hereward's initial attempts to clear up a run of mysteries that had troubled the village, but recently he had become more tolerant of their help, and Gwyneth found that she almost regarded him as a friend.

Hereward was looking doubtful. 'But we haven't any proof to give him, except something that Clem Ludel said when he was drunk. He's likely to deny it all when he's sober.'

'That's true,' Gwyneth agreed reluctantly. 'And that won't help Father Godfrey or Master Thorson to recapture the prisoners. We don't have a clue who the Hoodman is. Practically everyone in Glastonbury wears a hood.'

'Even Father Godfrey,' said Hereward, with a faint grin.

In spite of her anxiety, Gwyneth smiled back at him. Their days of suspecting Father Godfrey of every crime in the village were well and truly over.

'For that matter,' Hereward went on, 'we don't even know that the Hoodman is in Glastonbury. Clem Ludel didn't say where he had met him. He could be based in Wells, or Bath, or Bristol, or over the border in Wales. Even in the forest somewhere. We need to find out more before we tell anyone.'

'Then that's what we'll do,' Gwyneth said determinedly. 'We can't have the village full of traitors, just when everything's so peaceful. We'll find the Hoodman, and then tell Master Thorson or Father Godfrey.'

Even as her words died away, she knew how difficult that would be. The Hoodman was dangerous, a fighting man and a traitor, while she and Hereward had no idea of where to start looking for him.

All the same, she promised herself, *we have to try*.

Gwyneth closed the kitchen door firmly behind her, shutting out the icy winter wind, and set her empty basket on the table. It was the morning after Master Ludel's drunken disclosure, and she and Hereward had just returned from taking breakfast to the stonemasons at the abbey.

'I must go up and speak to Mistress le Fevre,' Gwyneth said to her mother, who stood at the table kneading bread dough. 'Uncle Owen gave me a message for her. Aunt Anne is ill, and won't be able to come in to work on the vestments today.'

'Your aunt is ill?' Idony paused in her work, looking up with an expression of concern on her face. 'I hope it's nothing serious.'

'No, just a cold,' Gwyneth replied, hanging her cloak on its hook behind the door.

'Then I'll make her a bowl of my barley

cordial,' said Idony, 'and you can take it over there later. For now, get you up to Mistress le Fevre, and ask her if you can help her instead.'

Gwyneth was delighted to do as her mother asked. She was very fond of the sensitive embroideress; though Mistress le Fevre had been quite ill since coming to the Crown, after the terrifying experience of seeing Lady Isabelle Carfax drown, she was still dedicated to her work. Gwyneth would never tire of feasting her eyes on the beautiful things Marion created for the abbey. Maybe Aunt Anne's absence was her chance to learn how to make something just as beautiful.

She ran up the stairs and tapped on Mistress le Fevre's door. The embroideress's gentle voice bid her enter. Inside the room was warm and bright, with tapers burning and a fire blazing in the hearth. Marion le Fevre was seated at her embroidery frame by the window, her needle poised in her hand as she turned to look at Gwyneth.

'Ah, poor Anne,' she said when Gwyneth relayed her message. 'I trust she will be well soon. If you see her you must give her my good wishes.'

'Mother said I might help you instead,' Gwyneth told her hopefully.

Marion le Fevre smiled. 'Yes, there is a task that you could do for me. Come over to the table and I'll show you.'

She placed a sheet of fine vellum in front of Gwyneth, with a picture of entwined leaves and flowers drawn upon it.

'Take this needle,' she said, 'and make holes along the line of the drawing, very evenly . . . like this. Can you manage that, my dear?'

'Yes.' Gwyneth sat down and took the needle, puzzled what use the task might be. The vestments in the abbey weren't made of vellum!

'I shall lay the drawing on the fabric,' Mistress le Fevre went on, exactly as if Gwyneth had asked her out loud, 'and scatter powdered chalk along the lines. The chalk will pass through the holes and so make a picture of the design on the fabric. We call it pouncing.'

'I see!' Gwyneth beamed up at her. 'What a clever idea!'

Mistress le Fevre gave her musical laugh. 'Not mine, dear child. But I have been well taught.'

She returned to the embroidery frame and

began to stitch again. Gwyneth stabbed carefully at the vellum, making sure that the holes were evenly spaced. It was bliss to sit in Marion le Fevre's warm room, and even more to think that she was making a contribution, however small, to the holy things which the embroideress was making for the abbey.

After a while she lifted her head and glanced over to see what Mistress le Fevre was working on. A length of golden silk was stretched on her frame, and along one side of it Marion was embroidering a magnificent dragon, all scarlet coils and raking claws, with flame spouting from its mouth.

'That's wonderful!' Gwyneth exclaimed. 'Is it to be an altar cloth?'

'Yes,' Marion replied. 'Over here—' she gestured to the blank space on the silk—'will be Michael the Archangel, battling against the dragon.'

The writhing shape reminded Gwyneth of something. Why should it make her think of mud and rust? she wondered. Then it came to her: she had seen the same design on the hilt of the old sword that Hereward had found the day before! It was so rusty that she had not realized until now that it must be a dragon.

'The sword,' she whispered, and added more loudly, 'Hereward's sword!'

Marion le Fevre looked up enquiringly.

'Hereward found a sword with a dragon on it,' Gwyneth explained.

'A sword, you say?' For a moment Mistress le Fevre was frozen into stillness, her needle halfway through the fabric. Then she laughed. 'With a dragon? Well, there must be many such designs around Glastonbury. Was not the dragon the emblem of King Arthur?'

'Of course . . .' Gwyneth breathed, with the familiar shiver of delight when she thought of the legends which twined around the village. Glastonbury had once been known as Avalon, where King Arthur had come after his last battle to be healed of his wounds, and all the stories said that one day he would return. Gwyneth had seen his warriors sleeping in an enchanted cave under the Tor, so she knew that the legends must be true. A sudden shock ran through her and she almost dropped her needle as she remembered that she had seen the design on the embroidery frame not just once before: the dragon wreathed in thorns had also been cut into the rock that covered the entrance to the cave where the warriors slept.

For a wild moment she wondered if Hereward's sword had once belonged to King Arthur himself. Almost as quickly, she scolded herself for being so fanciful. It could not be that old or Master Brockfield, or his forebears, would surely have found it before now. Besides, there must be many swords in Glastonbury with the sign of the dragon, in memory of Arthur, just as Mistress le Fevre said.

Gwyneth looked back at Marion, eager to ask her if she had seen any swords like it, but the embroideress had begun to stitch busily once more. 'I hope Hereward will take care with his sword,' was all that she said. 'Such weapons can be dangerous.'

Hereward trudged along the village street, his head down into the wind. His cloak was clutched tightly about him, not just to keep out the cold, but also to conceal the sword which he had furtively retrieved from its hiding place.

His mother had sent him to Tom Smith's forge to collect a pot-hook she had ordered a few days before. Hereward had brought the sword with him, still wrapped in its sackcloth; he wanted to show it to Tom Smith, who might be glad to clean the rust off the blade and beat it into shape when he saw how wonderful it was. Then, Hereward thought, it would cut even better; it would be a weapon worthy of the greatest warrior, perhaps even one of Arthur's knights.

A tuneless whistling was coming from the forge as Hereward approached, punctuated by the sound of hammer blows. When Hereward went inside he saw that Tom Smith was not there; it was his brother Hywel who stooped over the anvil, hammering at something small held in a pair of long-handled tongs. Firelight from the hearth shone on his face and fair curly hair.

Hywel glanced up at the sound of the opening door, and for an instant it looked as if he was expecting to see someone else. He seemed disappointed to see Hereward standing there, but the expression lasted only a moment before a welcoming smile spread over the smith's broad face.

'Hereward, good morrow! Are you here for your mother's pot-hook? I'm just finishing it now.'

He gave the piece of iron a couple more blows, and doused it in a nearby bucket of water to cool the metal in its new shape. Steam hissed into the air, and Hywel held up the hook for Hereward to admire.

'There! That'll hold many a pot safely,' he said.

'Thank you, Master Hywel,' said Hereward, taking it and handing Hywel a coin in return. As he opened his pouch, the sword slipped out from under his arm.

'What have you got there?' Hywel asked, his blue eyes round with curiosity.

Hereward hesitated. If Tom Smith had been there he could have asked him to work on the sword without telling anyone, and the good-natured smith might have agreed. His brother was just as good-natured, but he was quite incapable of keeping a secret. By nightfall the whole of Glastonbury would know that Hereward Mason had found a sword.

But Hywel was already stooping to pick up the

weapon and unfolding its sackcloth wrappings. ''Tis a sword!' he exclaimed. 'Are you going to be a knight, Hereward?'

Hereward forced a smile. 'No, Master Hywel. I was just hoping Tom might clean it up a bit.'

The smith's eyes gleamed as he ran his hand over the rusty blade. 'I'll be glad to do it for you.'

'But I can't pay you,' said Hereward. 'I'm sorry.'

'No matter.' Hywel grasped the hilt with one huge hand in its protective leather glove. 'I'll work on it for you and welcome—'twill be good practice, if naught else.' His eyes shone and he looked around as if he could see ranks of half-finished weapons, waiting his craft.

Hereward felt a stir of curiosity. Why should Hywel need practice in working on a sword? The forge in Glastonbury worked mostly on tools and farm implements, for only Finn Thorson among the village folk regularly carried a sword.

'Thank you, Master Hywel,' he replied, grateful that Hywel did not seem curious about where the sword had come from, though he felt a possessive twinge when he saw his blade in someone else's hands.

Carefully Hywel took up a whetstone and began to burnish the rust from the blade. Hereward held his breath as the metal started to gleam, firelight reflecting down the length of it until the sword itself looked like a slice of flame.

'Aye, I'll be doing more of this soon,' Hywel remarked, shooting a look of suppressed excitement at Hereward. 'But I mustn't speak of it,' he added with a flash of alarm in his eyes.

'Please, Master Hywel.' Hereward was even more curious now. 'I won't tell anyone, I promise, if you don't tell anyone about my sword. We . . . we can share a secret, one with the other, can we not?'

'Well . . .' Hywel set the whetstone on one side and squinted down the blade; light rippled on it like water and it was an effort for Hereward to tear his eyes away and focus on the smith. 'A great lord's man came to me the other day. I'm to go and work for him, but I mustn't tell, because the lord doesn't want his enemies to know how many weapons and men he has.' His face shone with innocent pride. 'His man said he wants the most skilful smith hereabouts.'

But surely that would be Tom, not Hywel?

Hereward thought uneasily, knowing the different skills the two brothers possessed. Something about the story didn't ring true—not that Hereward suspected Hywel of telling falsehoods, but it seemed likely that whoever had asked for his labour had some less honourable reason behind his request. It wasn't hard to deceive Hywel, and probably someone had been flattering him to persuade him to work for nothing.

'That's good news, Master Hywel,' he said politely. 'Does that mean you'll be leaving the village?'

'Oh, I'd not leave Tom for good.' Hywel sounded shocked. 'But I'm to go away for a few days, right enough. The lord's man will come and tell me when. Now,' he went on, giving the sword an experimental swing, 'we'll put a real good edge on that.'

He blew up the fire with a pair of bellows and thrust the sword into its depths, drawing it out when the blade glowed red to lay it on the anvil. He took up a hammer and aimed a blow, and Hereward braced himself for the deafening ring of iron against iron.

But when the hammer struck the blade there

was a sharp crack, and the solid square head sheared completely into two. One piece buried itself in the wall beside Hywel; Hereward ducked as the second whistled over his head and landed with a clatter on the flagstones behind him.

'By Our Lady!' Hywel breathed out, staring at the sword. 'That hammer was naught but a week old—new, but tried and tested. That's a blade indeed.'

Hereward gazed in disbelief at the glowing length of metal. He had known the blade must be sharp when it cut through the hawthorn boughs by the river, but he had never imagined any sword could break a hammer like that. He felt a surge of pride that he had found such a weapon.

'Here, take it.' Hywel thrust the hilt into Hereward's hand as if he thought the dragon was going to come to life and bite him. 'Take it away. I can't work a blade like that, whatever the lord's man may say about me. There's something unchancy about it.' With a bewildered look at the hammer handle, which he still clutched in his other hand, he added, 'What Tom will say about this, I don't know.'

Hereward bundled up the sword in its sack-cloth wrappings again and hid it under his cloak. The blade was clean, and clearly needed no sharpening, so his instincts told him to keep it out of sight once more. Thanking Hywel, he headed out into the street again.

'Have a care!' the smith called after him. 'That sword is dangerous!'

Chapter Five

Gwyneth blew out the taper and rolled herself in her blankets, trying to ignore the icy draughts that blew through the gaps in the window shutters. At the other side of their attic bedroom, Hereward was already snoring.

Gwyneth sighed; she had wanted to discuss things with him. Hereward had been busy with errands of his own all day; the only time they had been together had been at meals, when their father and mother were with them. There had been no chance to talk further about the Hoodman, and what they might do to discover his identity.

Closing her eyes, Gwyneth told herself that tomorrow would have to do. But she could not help wondering what plans the Hoodman was making at that very moment to put Henry of Truro on the throne, and whether the loss of a day would mean that they had lost the chance of stopping him. What would happen to her beloved home if the Hoodman and his men over-ran the village?

She was drifting into sleep when a noise roused her. Her eyes flew open, but she could see nothing except the blankets mounded over the sleeping Hereward, faintly outlined in the moonlight that leaked through the shutters. She was just deciding that the noise had been nothing more than the creak of a floorboard settling when she heard it again, and more clearly: the soft sound of move-ment outside her bedroom door. A moment later the door began to edge open.

Gwyneth lay frozen, sure that the pounding of her heart must be loud enough to wake the whole inn. Her mother and father would not creep in like this, and the servants, Wat and Hankin, would have knocked first. She closed her eyes again, leaving only the narrowest slit so that she could see through the fringe of her lashes.

A yellowish light filtered into the room, casting a narrow, triangular beam onto the floorboards. It came from a horn lantern, held in the hand of a tall figure muffled in a cloak. Once inside, the intruder halted and lifted his lantern high to look round. Gwyneth felt his gaze linger on her like the touch of a moth; it was the hardest thing she had ever done to lie still and breathe evenly, but she was determined he should believe she was asleep.

After a pause that seemed to last for a century, the intruder stole silently across the room, set down the lantern on the windowsill, and eased open the lid of the clothes chest that stood against the wall. He seemed to be searching for something, leaning over and stirring the clothes about with his free hand. While his head was well down over the chest Gwyneth pushed back her blankets and swung her feet to the floor, praying that the stranger would not hear her.

With her heart still thumping so hard she could scarcely draw breath, she crept towards the door. Once she reached the stairs, she could raise the alarm and have her father here in the blink of an eye.

But as she slipped into the passage, a hand shot out of the darkness behind the door, covering her mouth before she could utter a cry. A long, sinewy arm clamped about her chest. For a brief moment, panic turned Gwyneth's limbs to stone. Then she began to struggle furiously, kicking out backwards at her attacker. She felt her foot connect with his shin, and the man who held her let out a loud oath.

Through the open door Gwyneth saw the first intruder straighten up from the clothes chest. He grabbed the lantern and whirled round, and the yellow beam illuminated him from the waist up. He was someone Gwyneth had never seen before, powerfully built, with wiry black hair and beard.

'Silence, fool!' he hissed.

The noise had roused Hereward. Gwyneth watched as he loomed up in his bed with a blanket in both hands and flung it over the stranger's head. The man stumbled, groping at the heavy woollen folds, and dropped the lantern. At once the horn panels split apart and flames began to lick along the edges of the trailing bed cover.

Fear gave Gwyneth strength to twist her head to one side and free her mouth from the hand clamped over it. 'Help! Fire!' she screamed, trying to wrench herself free from the villain's grasp. 'Hereward, look out!'

For a brief moment the room was lit up with

lurid yellow light; then Hereward flung himself forward, smothering the flames with another blanket, and they were plunged into darkness again.

'Robbers!' Hereward yelled. 'Father! Help!'

His shouting, and the struggles of the man trapped in the blanket, soon roused the rest of the inn. Gwyneth heard a door crash open from further down the passage, where Wat and Hankin slept, while her father's voice came from below.

'Hereward? What's going on?'

'Thieves!' Gwyneth shouted, twisting like a snake against the arms that held her. 'Come quick!'

She heard her father calling urgently for a light, and rapid footsteps along the passage signalled the arrival of Wat and Hankin. Hankin's worried voice said, 'Gwyneth, lass?' Then there was a grunt, and her attacker abruptly released her. Gwyneth stumbled against the wall and leant there, shaking and catching her breath.

At first she could see nothing, and fear tightened its grip on her. The whole inn seemed to be filled with people blundering about in the darkness, shouting orders at each other. She heard Wat yell, 'Master Mason! I've caught one!' and then Hereward's angry voice replying, 'No, that's me! Get off.'

From the bedroom she heard a crash as the shutters were flung back, and the sound of someone scrambling out of the window onto the thatched roof of the outhouse below.

'I could have caught him if you hadn't grabbed me,' Hereward said bitterly to Wat.

At last Geoffrey Mason appeared up the stairs with a lamp in one hand and a pair of iron fire tongs in the other. In the lamplight Gwyneth saw Wat and Hereward standing together in the doorway of her room, while Hankin and another unknown man—presumably her attacker—wrestled together on the floor of the passage.

'Gwyneth, Hereward, get you down to your mother,' Geoffrey Mason snapped. 'Go to our bedroom and bar the door.'

Gwyneth hurried to obey and nearly fell headlong as the man fighting with Hankin suddenly heaved upright, tore himself free, and pushed past to reach the stairs ahead of her. Her father made a wild grab at him and tripped over Hankin, who was trying to stand up with his head bleeding from a knock. Geoffrey Mason almost overbalanced at the head of the stairs; the lamplight dipped and swirled.

The intruder vanished into the darkness below; a voice was raised in a loud challenge and there came another sound which sent Gwyneth's heart racing again: the clash of swords. She hesitated to obey her father now; it sounded more dangerous down there by far.

Then firelight lit the passage below as Idony Mason opened the door of her bedroom and looked out. Gwyneth caught a glimpse of a couple of dark forms heading for the stairs that led to the kitchen passage and the outer door of the inn, while yet another stranger fought with someone that Gwyneth recognized—Mistress le Fevre's manservant. He wielded his sword grimly and quietly, save for the stamping of his bare feet on the floor, steadily driving the intruder back towards the stairs.

'Hold him!' Geoffrey Mason shouted from behind Gwyneth. 'We need to question him.'

Another voice broke in before he had finished. 'No—no!' Venturing a few steps further down, Gwyneth saw that Marion le Fevre had emerged from her room, and was clinging to the door frame, half fainting. 'Help, I beg you!' she cried. 'Stand by me—protect me!'

Distracted by the conflicting orders, her servant glanced back, and his opponent took the chance to flee for the stairs. The servingman plunged after him. Gwyneth heard a door bang far below, followed by a flurry of galloping hooves that faded rapidly into silence.

The servingman returned, shaking his head. 'Your pardon, Master Mason,' he said. 'They're gone. They had horses in the yard. Shall I saddle up and follow?'

'You can try,' Gwyneth's father said. 'But I fear they'll be long gone.'

The man looked at his mistress for her orders, and Marion waved a slender white hand at him. 'Yes, try—if you're sure there are no more of them. But take care. I have great need of you here.'

The man gave her a curt nod and hurried off. Geoffrey Mason came down the attic stairs, holding his lamp high and staring round as if he expected to see more intruders lurking. What the lamplight showed was more doors opening along the passage, as the guests of the Crown cautiously poked their heads out to see if the uproar was really at an end.

'All is well,' Idony called to them. 'Go back to bed, I pray you.'

Slowly, the guests did as she asked. One man, a portly merchant, grumbled, 'What sort of inn is this, where honest folk can't lie quiet in their beds?' before he thumped his door shut again.

'He'll leave in the morning,' Idony predicted with a sigh.

'They must have broken in somewhere,' said Geoffrey Mason. 'Wat, Hankin, come with me and make sure all the doors are secure.'

The two servants followed him downstairs, and Hereward hurried after them. Gwyneth heard their footsteps going to and fro, and then the sound of the main door being locked and bolted. Her father and Hereward came back upstairs; Geoffrey was frowning, and Hereward had an odd, half-excited look on his face.

'What's the matter?' Gwyneth asked him.

It was her father who replied. 'They didn't break in. All the doors and windows are secure.'

'But that means someone inside must have let

them in!' Gwyneth could hardly believe it. 'No one would do that!'

'None of our household,' her mother agreed. 'But one of them could have been drinking in the taproom, and hid until everything was quiet before he let his fellows in. We don't go looking under every table or behind every barrel before we lock up.'

'We will in future,' Geoffrey Mason assured her grimly.

'Come, Mistress le Fevre,' said Idony, going down the passage to the embroideress who stood in her doorway, her face pale with shock. 'Let me see you back to bed. All's over now.'

'I shan't sleep a wink!' Marion protested, wringing her hands. 'What if those men come back?'

'They won't.' Gwyneth saw an exasperated look flit across her mother's face, but her voice was comforting. 'Get into bed, and I'll bring you a hot posset to help you sleep.'

Marion turned imploring eyes on her. 'And would your good Wat lie outside my chamber door?'

'If it will make you feel better,' Idony sighed.

Now that the excitement and danger were over, Gwyneth was beginning to shiver from cold, and when her mother ordered her and Hereward back to bed too, she did not protest.

'What on earth was all that about?' Hereward asked as they climbed the stairs. 'What did they want?'

'That first man was searching,' said Gwyneth, remembering the figure she had seen stooped over the chest beneath the window.

'But he can't have expected to find anything valuable in our room,' Hereward pointed out.

Their room was ice cold. Moonlight flooded in through the open shutters and the acrid smell of burning still lingered. Hereward pulled the half-burnt bedding off his bed and rolled it into a bundle.

Gwyneth waited until her brother had huddled into what remained of his bed-covers before she closed the shutters and groped her way to her own bed in the faint light that crept through the cracks.

'Father has money locked away,' she said, thinking aloud. 'But not enough to make it worth-while sending . . . how many men?'

'Four at least, maybe five.' Hereward gave an enormous yawn. 'And I'll tell you something else.'

Gwyneth jumped into bed and cocooned herself in the blankets. 'What?'

'I think I recognized one of them. I didn't get a good look, but he was very short and stocky. I think it was Osbert Teller.'

'What!' Gwyneth sat straight upright. 'It can't have been! Master Teller is working for Wasim Kharab now.'

She was not surprised by the idea that Osbert Teller, the dwarf who had once worked for Rhys Freeman, would be involved in robbery. After the trade in fake relics had been exposed, he had fled the village and taken a job with a Moorish merchant who travelled all over England. The last time Gwyneth and Hereward had seen him, he had been in Wells, one of the many towns Wasim visited with his covered wagon of exotic fare.

'He could have come back to Glastonbury,' Hereward pointed out. 'I'm sure it was him, really I am. You didn't see him—he ran along the passage while that other man had hold of you.'

Gwyneth lay down again, even more puzzled

than before. 'What could it mean?' she wondered out loud.

But a snore was the only answer Hereward gave her, and with that Gwyneth had to be content.

Idony Mason let Gwyneth and Hereward sleep late next morning. When they went down they found Mistress le Fevre and her manservant standing in the passage at the foot of the stairs. The man must have just returned from a fruitless search for the intruders, for he was still wearing his stained cloak and mud-spattered boots.

Gwyneth would not have believed the embroideress could look so angry. Her face was white and her hands clenched together like curved talons.

'Can you not follow orders, Master Hood?' she demanded.

'I did what I thought best.' The man's insolent tone shocked Gwyneth. 'Don't think you can keep me dangling at your girdle like a bunch of keys.'

'How dare you! Go—and take more care next time.'

With a face like thunder, the servingman spun round and strode out past Finn Thorson and Geoffrey Mason, who were examining the outer door. Marion also turned, drawing her breath sharply when she realized that Gwyneth and Hereward had overheard the quarrel. Her eyes were sparkling with tears as she brushed past them and fled into the kitchen.

Gwyneth watched her sympathetically. She had thought right from the first that Marion's man-at-arms was a surly fellow, and this only proved it. No servant worth his pay should be that discourteous, especially on the morning after his mistress had been so frightened in the night.

Hereward had walked down the passage to see what his father and the sheriff were doing; Gwyneth followed him.

'This is the way they came in,' Geoffrey Mason was saying as she drew near. 'But you'll see the lock and the bolts have not been damaged.'

'Someone must have let them in,' the sheriff agreed. 'You trust your servants?'

'Wat and Hankin?' Gwyneth's father frowned.

'Of course I do. They've worked for me for years. You know them yourself for honest men.'

Finn Thorson nodded. 'And you've no idea who these robbers were?'

'I didn't get a good look at them all,' Geoffrey explained. 'Those I did see, I didn't recognize. Mistress le Fevre's man tried to pursue them, but they had too good a start.'

'As well they did,' the sheriff commented. 'One man against so many—he was brave even to attempt it.'

Turning away from the door, he noticed Gwyneth and Hereward and wished them a curt good morrow. Hereward bowed in greeting while Gwyneth bobbed a curtsy, half wary that the sheriff had still not forgiven them for the trouble over the pig.

'Go in and have your breakfast,' said their father, herding them into the kitchen. 'Finn, come and take a mug of ale and tell me what you think of this business.'

Inside the kitchen Gwyneth was surprised to see Godfrey de Massard warming his hands at the fire while Idony stirred a pot of frumenty. Marion le Fevre sat at the kitchen table with her hands clasped round a mug of steaming cordial. Her anger had died away, leaving her pale and tired.

When their mother saw Gwyneth and Hereward, she fetched bowls from a shelf and spooned frumenty into them from the pot on the fire.

'Eat your breakfast,' she said briskly, setting the bowls on the table. 'And then you may be excused your tasks, after so much upset last night. Ivo and Amabel are waiting for you.'

'That's right,' said Finn Thorson, relaxing into a smile and soothing Gwyneth's fears that he still blamed them for the incident with the pig. 'They're off to the woods to cut green boughs for the Christmas feast, and they thought you would like to go with them.'

'Yes, please!' Gwyneth felt a grin spreading over her face. 'Hurry up, Hereward.'

Her brother spooned up his oatmeal without replying. He did not look as enthusiastic as Gwyneth expected; perhaps he was just tired after their disturbed night. He had lost half his blankets in the short-lived fire, so perhaps he had been too cold to rest properly.

While they were eating, Geoffrey fetched ale for the sheriff and Father Godfrey.

'I was with Master Thorson when your servant sent him word about the attack last night,' said the priest, explaining his presence. 'We were discussing what best to do about these escaped prisoners, if they should appear in Glastonbury. It seems more than coincidence that intruders should strike at this very time. Are you sure, Master Mason, that your night visitors were not some of these desperate men?'

'I'm not sure of anything.' Geoffrey Mason sounded harassed. 'But what would traitors want here at the Crown? What would anyone want, for that matter? We've naught worth stealing.'

'I doubt that, Master Mason,' Father Godfrey replied, smoothly courteous. 'Your inn is prosperous. And what of the expensive fabrics and threads that Mistress le Fevre is using? Would they not tempt a band of robbers?'

'Oh, sweet saints, no!' Marion le Fevre raised one white hand to her forehead, as if she had a headache. 'Say not so, Father Godfrey.'

The priest's grey eyes were chilly as he looked

at her. 'It would be foolish to ignore the possibility, mistress.'

Marion half rose to her feet and then sank back into her seat. 'Then I must have a guard on my room!' she demanded, her voice growing shrill. 'Especially when I am not there. Fabric and thread can be replaced, but what if robbers stole the holy altar cloths and vestments?'

Gwyneth shivered, sharing her dismay. She could hardly bear to think of robbers pawing over Mistress le Fevre's beautiful work, selling for gold what should have been given to the abbey in the name of God.

'We'll work something out.' Idony patted Marion gently on the shoulder. 'Drink your cordial, my dear; it will make you feel better.'

'I'll send one of my men,' Finn Thorson offered.

Marion thanked him distractedly and gulped some of the hot liquid, but neither the offer nor the cordial seemed to banish her fear. Her eyes were huge, as if she stared at some horror that no one else could see.

Looking at her, Gwyneth found her own apprehension reawakened. After the invasion the night before, the Crown was no longer the safe place it had once been; she couldn't think of anything she would like better than to get away from it for a while in the company of Ivo and Amabel Thorson, and stop thinking about robbers and traitors, or anything except preparing for the Yuletide festivities.

Chapter Six

When Hereward and Gwyneth left the kitchen, they found Ivo and Amabel waiting in the inn yard. Amabel was seated on the mounting-block, while Ivo was creeping up on one of Idony's chickens with a bucket in his hand, as if he were about to trap the chicken under it.

'Ivo!' Gwyneth called out sharply. 'Leave the chicken alone! Haven't you learnt *anything* from all the trouble over that pig?'

Hereward sighed. Gwyneth never missed an opportunity to tell him and Ivo how stupid they had been; he guessed it would be a long time before he heard the last of Master Brockfield's pig.

Ivo dropped the bucket while the chicken fluttered away, squawking, and swung round to face Gwyneth and Hereward with a wide grin on his face. 'I have to do something while we wait for you—slug-a-beds!'

'Well, we're ready now,' said Gwyneth. 'Where do you want to go?'

Amabel slid down from the mounting block. 'What about the woods near Chalcwelle?' she suggested. 'There's holly and ivy there in plenty.'

'All right.' Gwyneth did not look enthusiastic, and Hereward could guess why. Not long before, they had found the body of a man beside the spring, and more death had followed before they discovered the truth of how he died. Yet it would be stupid never to go into those woods again, so he nodded.

'Good.' Amabel gave a little skip. 'Will your father lend us your mule to carry the boughs back, do you think?'

'I'll ask,' Hereward offered. He slipped back into the kitchen, where his father was still in conference with Finn Thorson and Father Godfrey.

'Yes, take the mule and welcome,' Geoffrey Mason said when Hereward made his request. 'I shan't need it today.'

Hereward went to the stables to put a halter on the mule and panniers to hold the boughs. As he worked, he had time to think about an

81

idea that had lain at the back of his mind since he woke up, and by the time he led the mule out into the yard he knew what he meant to do.

'Here,' he said, handing the halter to Gwyneth. 'I'm not coming with you.'

'What?' Gwyneth looked half shocked, half irritated. 'Whyever not?'

'There's something else I want to do.'

'Playing with that stupid sword, I suppose,' his sister shot back at him.

'Sword? What sword?' asked Ivo, looking interested.

'Oh, Hereward found an old sword buried in the mud near Master Brockfield's pig shelter,' Gwyneth explained, with a scornful look at her brother.

Ivo's eyes lit up. 'A sword! Where is it? Can I see?'

'No, you can't,' Hereward said irritably, annoyed that Gwyneth had given away his secret. If Finn Thorson found out he had the sword it would certainly be taken away from him.

'It's only a rusty bit of iron,' Gwyneth said. 'I don't know why you're being so secretive about it. He'll hardly let me look at it,' she added to Ivo.

'Please come with us, Hereward,' Amabel begged. 'It won't be as much fun without you.'

Part of Hereward would have been happy to say yes, to go off and spend a carefree morning with his friends, but he knew that there was something more important he had to do. He shook his head determinedly.

'I don't know why you're being so rude and difficult,' his sister said crossly. Tugging at the mule's halter, she headed for the archway that led into the street, calling over her shoulder, 'Come on, you two. There's no point in arguing with him.'

Ivo and Amabel followed her. Looking back, Ivo said, 'Come and join us at Chalcwelle if you change your mind.'

Hereward grudgingly replied, 'All right,' but both he and Ivo knew that he didn't mean it.

Hereward breathed a sigh of relief as he left the last houses of the village behind him, and could take the sword from under his cloak where he had concealed it from prying eyes. Striding out more confidently, he took the road that led into the woods by the river.

Last night, when the robbers broke into the Crown, only Mistress le Fevre's manservant had wielded a proper weapon. His father had been prepared to fight with fire tongs, and Wat and Hankin had attacked the intruders with their bare hands, which had cost Hankin a blow to his head that had left his senses still dulled that morning. But now Hereward had a sword of his own, and all he needed was time to practise with it. If the men should return—which seemed likely, since they had been chased off empty-handed—he would be ready for them.

The marshy ground towards the river was growing hard with the winter cold; frost rimed the grass and the sprawling thickets of bramble and hazel. Only a few ragged leaves clung to the grey branches of the trees; fallen leaves crunched under Hereward's feet and the pools were iced over. The air was still, and he could hear nothing but the thin piping of a few hungry birds.

Leaving the path, he wound his way between

the trees and clumps of dead bracken until he reached a clearing where he could practise undisturbed. He raised the sword, admiring the way the new-cleaned blade gleamed in the pale daylight. He could not forget how Hywel Smith's hammer had flown in two; while part of him was sure that the hammer must have been faulty, he secretly hoped that it had been the power of the sword.

'Sir Hereward of Glastonbury,' he murmured, imagining that he could hear cheering crowds around him as he took the prize in a tournament.

Then he shook his head, half ashamed. He was starting to think like Gwyneth, who always had some dream or other in her head. He preferred to be more practical. He might never be a knight, but any more intruders at the Crown would get a nasty shock.

He swung the sword at the overhanging branch of a tree. The blade sheared through the wood as if there were no obstacle at all in its way, and the branch thudded softly to the ground. The hammer—or the sword?

At that moment, Hereward heard the crisp sound of approaching footsteps, and he shrank back into the shelter of the tree's ivy-covered trunk.

The newcomer was Ursus. When he came level with Hereward he paused and glanced round, as if the noise of the falling branch had alerted him. Part of Hereward wanted to step out and greet him; he and Gwyneth saw the hermit so seldom that it was hard to miss the chance of talking to him. Yet his instinct to keep the sword a secret was stronger. He stayed in hiding, and after a moment Ursus walked on, his brown habit quickly disappearing among the trees.

Hereward emerged from behind his tree and gripped the sword two-handed as he began to practise again. He tried to remember the stance of Mistress le Fevre's servant, and how the man had controlled his weapon. He was a true swordsman, Hereward had seen that for himself, skilful and brave. Hereward wondered if he dared ask the man for lessons. But he was grim and unfriendly, and besides, it would mean revealing the secret of the sword.

Swinging the blade energetically, Hereward started to grow warm, and his breath puffed out in a cloud in the frosty air. He was concentrating so hard that at first he did not hear the sound of more footsteps drawing closer through the trees. When he did, the men were almost upon him—two or three, Hereward guessed, catching the murmur of voices.

Once again he slipped into the shelter of the tree, suppressing a sigh of exasperation. At this rate, he might as well have done his sword practice in the market-place! For a few moments he listened, trying to breathe silently, with a rivulet of sweat trickling down his nose, and sweat prickling on his back where he did not dare move to scratch it.

Then the men walked past his hiding-place, and Hereward almost cried out loud in surprise. There were three of them, and the man in the centre was Hywel Smith. A blindfold covered the smith's eyes, and he shuffled along hesitantly as if he was afraid of tripping. The men on either side of him each had a hand on his arm, guiding him.

'Easy does it, Master Smith,' one of them said. 'Lift your feet, there's a branch just here. That's right.'

'Is it much further?' Hywel asked.

'No, not far,' the man reassured him.

Hereward recognized the voice, and when the man glanced round he knew his face, too; it was Clem Ludel, the stonemason who had spoken so loudly of treason, and tried to recruit Matt Green into the Hoodman's army.

His heart pounding, Hereward shrank back among the ivy stems. Even with the sword in his hand, he did not want to be discovered. But as the men drew away from him he slid stealthily out of his hiding-place and followed.

After a while he began to breathe more easily. Tracking the men was not difficult. They were concentrating too hard on guiding Hywel to have any thought for who might be coming up behind them, and Hereward had spent enough time in these woods to know how to tread silently. He managed to keep them in sight while slipping from tree to tree for concealment, as they led him deep into the heart of the forest.

The trees grew more thickly here, and their leafless branches cut off the light from the sky. Hereward began to worry that his quarry would escape him in the gloom. Then he heard the sounds of more men from somewhere up ahead:

a voice raised, shouting orders, the whinny of a horse, the crackling of a fire.

The noises grew louder, until Hereward found himself standing on the edge of a clearing. What he saw was so unexpected that all he could do was stand and stare, the sword loose in his hand. Tents had been set up in a circle under the surrounding trees, with a few sturdier shelters at the edge, roughly built of planks or interwoven boughs. Not far to his left, horses and a couple of mules were tethered in a line.

In the centre of the clearing was a fire with a pair of cooking pots suspended from a framework of branches lashed together. One man was crouched beside it, stirring a steaming, meat-scented broth. Further away from the fire, three or four groups of men were practising with swords, while a few of their companions sat close to the flames with ale mugs in their hands, offering encouragement or mockery in equal measure.

Clem Ludel and the other man guided Hywel into the clearing, and Master Ludel pulled off the blindfold. The smith blinked, looking around him with a puzzled expression on his face.

'What's this? Where have you brought me?'

The other man patted his shoulder. 'Don't you worry none, Master Smith. Our lord keeps this camp in the woods so his enemies don't see his preparations for war.'

Hywel smiled and nodded, as if the explanation satisfied him. But it didn't satisfy Hereward. This wasn't the way great lords went about the art of warfare. They had armoured knights on splendid horses, not this ragged bunch of men and the sorry nags lined up at the edge of the clearing.

Master Ludel led Hywel across the open ground to a tent on the far side, while his companion retreated to the fire and said something to the man bent over the cooking pots. The man by the fire straightened up, and Hereward got a proper look at him for the first time.

It was Osbert Teller! Hereward drew in his breath sharply. Suddenly it seemed possible that the dwarf had been one of the robbers who attacked the Crown the night before. But what was he doing here, and who were these men? Could they be the Hoodman's traitorous army? And what could they want from the Crown Inn?

His mind was racing so fast that for a moment Hereward stopped being vigilant. He suddenly realized that Osbert Teller had got up from the fire. Paralysed by shock, he stared in dismay as the dwarf trotted across the clearing, straight towards him.

Chapter Seven

Snapping back to life, Hereward dived for the bushes, where he crouched with the sword gripped at the ready. His whole body tingled with fear. Through the branches he saw Osbert Teller pull open the flap of the nearest tent and go inside, paying no attention to the figure hiding in the undergrowth. Limp with relief, Hereward listened to him moving around inside and then saw him leave with a small closed box in his hands.

A stench was rising from the ground at Hereward's right, and he realized with disgust that he had chosen to hide in the place where the men had dug the trench for their privy. Edging away from it, more careful this time to stay under cover, he peered out again into the camp.

Osbert Teller was back at the fire, scattering something from the box into one of the cooking pots. Then he took a bowl, filled it, and handed it to Ludel's companion. Hereward glanced around to see if Wasim Kharab was here too, but there was no sign of the Moorish merchant or his mule-cart.

'Hey, Osbert! Come here!'

The shout came from the other side of the clearing. A man strode out into the open, and once again Hereward froze with shock. Tall, with cropped russet hair and a brown cloak: it was Marion le Fevre's servingman!

Hereward's mind whirled as he watched the man point across the clearing to where Hywel Smith stood with Clem Ludel. He could not begin to understand what was happening, nor how the man came to be here. The last time he had seen him, he had been telling his mistress, Marion le Fevre, that he had failed to catch up with the intruders who broke into the Crown.

'Build a fire for the smith,' the man ordered Osbert. 'Then you can bring the weapons that need repairing, and work the bellows for him.'

The dwarf looked up, and even at that distance Hereward made out the grumpy expression on

93

his face. 'But I'm cooking your dinner, master,' he protested.

The man gave him a rough push in Hywel's direction. 'You'll take any excuse to laze around, Osbert. Do as I bid you, or you'll feel my dagger.'

Osbert Teller looked terrified. 'No call for that, Master Hood. I'm going.' He shambled off, past Hywel, and began hefting logs from a pile under the trees.

Another shock thrilled through Hereward. Master Hood! Like Gwyneth, he had forgotten the name of Mistress le Fevre's servingman. They had met the man so briefly, and so many weeks ago. But now he recalled how the embroideress had addressed him that morning, and he remembered his name: Galfridas Hood.

Hereward swallowed as fear rose within him on frantic wings. This was the army of traitors Master Ludel had spoken of, the escaped prisoners from Bristol who meant to overthrow King Richard and put Henry of Truro in his place. Galfridas Hood must be the leader Ludel had spoken of: the Hoodman! While his mistress was distracted making altar cloths in Glastonbury, he had forged a different career for himself, one that served a very different master.

Hereward's first instinct was to flee. The hard metal hilt of the sword gripped in his hand helped him to think more calmly—as a true knight would, he told himself. He had to stay, and watch, and learn all he could so that he could take the news back to the village and the traitors could be captured once more.

The Hoodman was gathering his men around him. Hereward dropped flat on his stomach and wormed his way forward, still clutching the sword, until he lay on the very edge of the trees, concealed behind a clump of dead bracken. From here he could see better, and hear everything that Galfridas Hood was saying.

'Disguises will be ready for us,' he told his men. 'Surcoats with King Richard's coat of arms, so that everyone will take us for his guard. We can walk unchallenged into the Palace of Westminster, and there we'll seize power. There are none there strong enough to stop us.'

There were murmurs from the men clustered around him, some approving, others more doubtful. The man who had accompanied Hywel and Ludel spoke up. 'How do we know we're strong enough, master?'

Galfridas Hood turned towards him, his unmatched eyes like chips of coloured ice. 'Because the fools will take us for their friends until it's too late,' he replied. 'And because I know of something that will help us, something that will make it all too easy to claim the throne.'

Mystified, Hereward wondered what that might be. Master Hood did not explain any more, and the little he had said seemed to satisfy his men.

'What about my lord Henry?' one of them asked. 'When will he come to take his rightful place?'

Something about the question angered Galfridas Hood. His eyes narrowed and his voice had a hard edge as he replied, 'When the time is right, fool.' He gave a curt nod. 'Very well, get to your tasks.'

The men began to move off in ones and twos. Hereward waited in case he could learn more, but soon he realized that with the traitors moving around, the chances of his being discovered were much greater. As silently as he could he wriggled backwards until he was concealed in the thickets again. Then he got to his feet and fled towards Glastonbury.

Hereward pelted through the market-place, ignoring Margery Carver who called out a greeting to him as he passed by. His heart was thumping and his breath came in noisy gasps. When he gained the inn yard he paused, chest heaving. He had already decided what he must do. First, hide the sword. Then find Gwyneth and tell her everything he had discovered. Together, they would go to find Finn Thorson or Father Godfrey, and give them the news of the traitors' camp in the woods.

When he went into the kitchen, his mother was sealing the pastry lid on a veal pie. 'I thought you went to the woods with Gwyneth and the Thorson twins,' she said. 'Gwyneth has been home this half hour.'

'Where is she?' Hereward panted. 'I have to talk to her.'

Idony looked up with a flicker of surprise, but she did not question the urgency in his tone. 'Helping Mistress le Fevre,' she replied.

Hereward pounded up the stairs, only to pause in the passage outside Mistress le Fevre's room. He had just seen her servingman at the head of the army of traitors. Did the embroideress have any idea what Galfridas Hood was doing? At any rate, Hereward decided, he could not risk telling his news where Mistress le Fevre could hear him.

He rapped on the door and flung it open. Stepping into the room, he stared in disbelief at a new piece of fabric that was stretched on Mistress le Fevre's embroidery frame: a length of scarlet linen, with a fierce golden lion stitched on it. Gwyneth, seated on a stool beside the fire, had another length spread across her lap, and she was busily hemming it with her head bowed. Hereward's heart twisted with horror as one more piece of the puzzle fell into place. The golden lion was part of King Richard's coat of arms. Marion le Fevre and his sister were stitching the surcoats that the traitors would use for their disguise!

Gwyneth looked up irritatedly. 'Hereward, do you have to bang about like that?'

Hereward ignored her peevish tone. 'I have to speak to you.'

'What for? Can't you see I'm busy?'

'This is important, Gwyneth. I've something to tell you, *now*.'

His sister held her needle poised as if she couldn't wait to take another stitch. 'What is it, then?'

'Come out here,' said Hereward, beckoning to her. It took all his self-control not to start shouting. Why did Gwyneth have to be so difficult?

Gwyneth sighed and rolled her eyes in exasperation. Before she could reply, Marion le Fevre said gently, 'You had better go with Hereward, my dear. You know he won't give up until you do.'

Reluctantly Gwyneth laid the length of fabric aside, got up and came to Hereward at the door. Hereward closed the door and took her by the wrist, none too gently, drawing her down the passage as far as the head of the stairs, well out of earshot of Marion le Fevre.

'God's bones, Hereward, what is it?' Gwyneth demanded, pulling her wrist free and rubbing it where his fingers had left red marks.

'What are those things you're sewing?' Hereward asked her.

'What?' Gwyneth's voice was sharp with anger. 'Have you dragged me out here just to ask me that?'

'No, of course not. Listen.' Hereward took a deep breath and told her what he had seen in the forest, how he had followed the blindfolded smith to the traitors' camp, and overheard the plot to storm the Palace of Westminster and seize the throne for Henry of Truro.

'Galfridas Hood was there,' he finished. 'Mistress le Fevre's servingman. He's the Hoodman that Clem Ludel spoke of! And those surcoats you're making are so the traitors can disguise themselves as King Richard's guards.'

Gwyneth's response astounded him. Instead of sharing his dismay, she burst into a peal of merry laughter. 'Hereward, you are stupid!' she exclaimed when she could speak again. 'They're not traitors, they're mummers.'

'What?' Hereward stared at her.

'Those folk in the forest, they're a company of mummers. They're coming here, to the Crown, to perform their play at New Year. Mistress le Fevre is helping them with their costumes.'

Hereward felt as if he had just taken a step in

the dark and found nothing under his feet. For a moment he considered whether Gwyneth could be right, and he had completely mistaken what he had seen. Then he remembered how Galfridas Hood had addressed his men.

'They were plotting treason,' he insisted. 'I heard Master Hood giving them their orders.'

Gwyneth wiped her eyes with the corner of her apron; her face was flushed with laughter. 'They were practising their play, Hereward.'

'No, they weren't.' Fury had banished Hereward's astonishment by now, making him all the more certain. 'I was there; you weren't. I know what I heard. Why would they blindfold Hywel Smith if they're only mummers?'

'Because if Hywel knew where to find them he would show the whole village. You know very well that he can't keep a secret.' Gwyneth turned away. 'I must get on with my work.'

'No, wait.' Added to the chaos of Hereward's other feelings was a genuine fear for what Gwyneth was getting mixed up with. 'You can't go back in there. What if Mistress le Fevre knows about the traitors? Galfridas Hood is her servant.'

'*What?*' Gwyneth faced him again, her green

eyes hot with anger. 'Are you accusing Mistress le Fevre now? Even if they *were* traitors—which they aren't—she wouldn't have anything to do with it. You know how gentle she is. She only wants to make beautiful things for the abbey.'

Hereward hesitated, wretchedly aware that what Gwyneth said was true. Or at least, he reminded himself, it was what they had always believed to be true.

'I still don't think—' he began.

'No, you don't think!' Gwyneth interrupted. Her voice rose to a shout. 'You're stupid and ridiculous. Just because we found out things before, you think everything's a mystery. You're worse than Father Godfrey, seeing traitors everywhere.'

Down below, the kitchen door opened. 'What are you two doing?' Idony's voice came up the stairs. 'I should think the whole village can hear you.'

'It's Hereward,' Gwyneth replied. Her eyes were sparkling with tears of anger. 'He keeps saying that—'

'I'll have no tale-telling,' her mother retorted. 'Gwyneth, why are you not helping Mistress le

Fevre? Hereward, come down here. I have an errand for you.'

With a look of childish glee, Gwyneth stuck out her tongue at Hereward before flouncing off down the passage to Mistress le Fevre's room.

Desperately, Hereward called after her, 'Don't tell her—' only to break off as the door to the bedchamber snapped shut. For a moment he stared at the oaken panels. Suppose Gwyneth did tell Mistress le Fevre that he had discovered the camp in the forest? If the embroideress was a traitor, what might she do to them both?

'Hereward!' his mother called again.

Hereward could do nothing but obey. When he went downstairs his mother was waiting for him by the kitchen door.

'Run to Master Brockfield's,' she instructed him, 'and ask him when he will deliver the geese I have ordered for the Christmas feasting. If you hurry you'll be back in time for dinner.'

'But I have to do something!' Hereward protested, knowing how urgent it was to find Finn Thorson or Father Godfrey and tell them what he had discovered.

'Do as you're bid,' Idony snapped. 'Hasn't there

been enough trouble about that pig, without you causing more now? Do you think guests will want to stay in an inn where there are such unruly children?' She whirled round and retreated to the kitchen.

Sighing, Hereward trailed out to the inn yard, but as soon as he reached the street his pace quickened. The best he could do now was to finish his errand as fast as he could, and then go in search of Master Thorson.

The villagers crowded around the stalls in the market-place, shopping for honey or spices or other treats for Yuletide. On the other side of the street a group of grey-clad pilgrims were entering the abbey grounds, summoned by the chapel bell that rang for the mid-day service of sext. The village looked so peaceful and ordinary; it was almost impossible to believe that not far away a traitorous plot was being hatched, with swords new-forged by the local smith to be raised against the king. Part of Hereward wanted to accept Gwyneth's explanation that it was all meant for a New Year mumming, but he could not consider that seriously. And nor would Gwyneth, if she had seen what he had.

The path to John Brockfield's cottage took Hereward close to the ferry. As he approached, he heard angry voices ahead. He ducked down, hoping to slip past, guessing that someone was arguing with Bryan the ferryman about the fare. Then his stomach lurched as he recognized the voices: one was Bryan's, the other belonged to Galfridas Hood.

Everything in Hereward wanted to continue on his errand and pretend he had not heard. But almost without his willing it, his feet turned aside into the undergrowth beside the path, so that he could creep up to the ferry unobserved.

Bryan was standing on the river bank beside his boat. Galfridas Hood was a pace or two away, one hand on the hilt of his sword, his face set in lines of cold anger.

'I know they were your men,' Bryan was saying, his lanky frame leaning threateningly towards Master Hood. 'I've seen you with them, more than once. And I want to know what they were doing leading Hywel Smith blindfold. Were they playing a trick on him?'

'How should I know?' The Hoodman waved a hand dismissively. 'If it was a jest, what of it?'

'It's no jest to lead away a lad like Hywel,' Brian retorted. 'He'll trust anyone. Easy to make him the butt for cheap laughter, maybe, but you'll not do that while he has friends to look out for him.'

'Will we not?' The Hoodman's voice had changed; the softness of it sent a shiver through Hereward and he found himself thinking of Wasim Kharab's snake, Yasmin. Galfridas Hood took a silent pace forward, sliding a dagger from his belt, and before Hereward could move he plunged it deep into the ferryman's stomach. Bryan's face sagged into a look of astonishment. He reached for Master Hood's throat as if he was about to grapple for his life, but his hands had no strength to grip. Hereward clamped his mouth shut on a horrified cry as the ferryman's body slumped forward, a scarlet stain blooming like a rose on the front of his tunic, and he crumpled to the ground at Master Hood's feet.

The Hoodman wrenched out the dagger, jabbing the body with his toe to make sure life had left it, and snatched up a handful of grass to clean the blood from the blade. Hereward backed away, his eyes fixed on the ferryman's motionless body. But he stumbled over a stone, and instantly Galfridas Hood whipped round.

'Who's there?' he called.

Hereward turned and fled, hearing the sounds of pursuit behind him. He tried to run quietly, weaving through the trees in an attempt to throw Master Hood off his trail, but fear and the horror of what he had just seen blinded his eyes and made him clumsy. He knew that the Hoodman would be able to follow his blundering progress like a hound pursuing a wounded deer.

Ducking behind a bramble thicket, Hereward tried to catch his breath, his ears straining to discover where his enemy was now.

'Ursus!' He dared not call aloud; instead his voice came out as a rough whisper. 'Ursus, where are you? Help me!'

As if in answer to his plea, a hand fell on his shoulder. Hereward spun round, but his gasp of relief became a cry of terror as he found himself looking up into the cold, mismatched eyes of Galfridas Hood.

'Interfering brat!' growled the Hoodman.

'I don't know what you mean!' Hereward protested in vain. The next instant the world grew dark as the stifling folds of a sack fell over his head, blotting out the forest around him like the blink of a gigantic eye.

Chapter Eight

'. . . *for wickedness lies buried, And evil flees away.*'

Marion le Fevre's sweet voice filled the room as she sang over her stitching. Gwyneth listened, enchanted. It was ridiculous of Hereward to suggest that the embroideress might be involved with traitors! Gwyneth had said nothing to her about his accusations, because she knew how upset the sensitive woman would be.

'*God has ordained a king, Desired by—*' Marion began the next verse, only to break off as a knock came at the door.

Not Hereward again! Gwyneth thought impatiently.

But when the door opened, her mother was standing there. 'Gwyneth, dinner is ready,' she said, 'but Hereward isn't back from Master Brockfield's. We'll eat without him, and then if he still hasn't come you had better go to look for him.'

'Hereward is being *so* annoying,' said Gwyneth, tucking her needle through the linen so that she could find it easily later. 'I don't see why I should have to look for him, when I'm busy here.'

'You'll do as you're bid, young mistress.' Idony sounded harassed. 'How busy do you think I am with your tasks to do as well as my own?'

'Don't worry, Gwyneth.' Marion le Fevre reached out to touch her arm reassuringly. 'You can come back when you're ready, and if it pleases you I'll teach you that song. 'Twas made for King Richard's coronation,' she added to Idony. 'A worthy song for so noble a king.'

Gwyneth got up and bobbed a curtsy. 'Thank you, mistress. Would you like me to bring your dinner up to you? It's no trouble.'

'So kind . . .' Marion smiled at Gwyneth, her green eyes warm. 'You all take such good care of me!'

Once Gwyneth had served Mistress le Fevre, and helped her mother carry the guests' food through to the taproom, she ate her own meal. By the time she had finished, Hereward had still not returned. She stared out of the kitchen window, noticing that a few stray flakes of snow were drifting down, and thought regretfully of Marion le Fevre's cosy room.

'Gwyneth, stop daydreaming.' Her mother's voice was impatient again. 'Didn't I tell you to look for Hereward?'

'I'm just going,' Gwyneth said hastily, unhooking her cloak from behind the door.

By the time she reached the street, the snow was falling in a thin veil, melting as it touched the cobbles. The stallholders in the market-place were throwing sacks over their wares, while their few remaining customers made haste to complete their bargaining and hurry away. Gwyneth realized that she had a hole in her shoe and shivered as the icy snow-water soaked into her stocking.

When she passed the abbey gateway an unexpected flurry of snow almost blinded her, and she collided with a tall, dark figure who seemed to appear out of nowhere. Strong hands grasped her shoulders as her feet skidded on the wet ground, and held her until she regained her balance. She looked up into the smiling face of

Brother Timothy, a monk just a few years older than herself and Hereward.

'You're in a hurry,' he remarked as she thanked him.

'I'm looking for Hereward,' Gwyneth explained. 'He went to Master Brockfield's this morning, and he hasn't come back.'

Brother Timothy's long, bony face filled with concern. For a moment, Gwyneth could almost forget his new and deeply secret role as a Protector monk, dedicated to guarding the treasures of King Arthur until the time came for them to be revealed; now he looked more like her childhood friend again, the young lad who had climbed every tree in Glastonbury and outrun all the other village boys.

'There's nothing to worry about,' Gwyneth assured him, letting her exasperation show. 'Hereward just wants to go off by himself all the time.'

'I hope it is no more than that,' Brother Timothy agreed. 'If I see him, I will bid him go home at once.'

Gwyneth thanked him again and hurried on. As the path took her through the woods she kept her eyes open for Ursus, in case he had seen her brother. But there was no sign of the hermit.

When she approached the ferry, she heard the sound of voices. 'Hereward! Hereward!' she called.

The bushes by the path rustled, but it was not Hereward who emerged. Instead, it was Finn Thorson. His face was grim, and when Gwyneth hastened towards him he stretched out a hand to stop her.

'You can't go down there, Gwyneth,' he warned her. 'It's a sight not fit for your eyes.'

Gwyneth felt as if her heart had jumped into her throat. 'It's not . . . not Hereward, is it?'

The sheriff shook his head. 'No,' he reassured her. 'Hereward isn't there.' He paused and added, 'It's Bryan the ferryman. Someone has stabbed him.'

'He's dead?' Gwyneth gulped, staring up at him.

Finn Thorson nodded. 'Get you home now, Gwyneth,' he ordered. 'There's evil abroad.'

Not waiting to see if she would obey him, he turned and vanished back down the path that led to the ferry. Gwyneth hesitated. Her spine tingled as if the murderer was lurking behind her at that very moment, waiting to plunge his knife into her back. She wanted nothing more than to flee back to the safety of the Crown.

But stronger still was her anxiety about Hereward. She had to go on looking for him, more urgently than ever now that she knew what had happened to Bryan. Perhaps Hereward had not come home because he had met the murderer too. All her annoyance with him evaporated in a scorching wave of fear.

Struggling to think sensibly, she was about to set off again when John Brockfield appeared from the direction of the ferry.

'Master Brockfield!' she called. 'Have you seen Hereward?'

The farmer plodded up to her, his face deeply troubled. 'No,' he replied. 'Not since the two of you cleaned my pigs out.'

'But he came to see you!' Gwyneth exclaimed. 'Mother sent him on an errand.'

John Brockfield shook his head. 'I haven't seen him,' he repeated. Glancing back towards the ferry, he added, 'You know what's down yonder?'

Gwyneth nodded, mute with terror.

'I found the poor dead soul when I went to take the ferry over to my pigs,' the farmer told her. 'But I don't reckon it's aught to do with Hereward. Like as not he met that other young limb, Ivo, and they went off to play. You'd best get home, and ask your father to go and look for him.' He patted Gwyneth comfortingly on the shoulder, and turned back towards his own cottage.

Gwyneth began to retrace her steps towards the Crown, trying to convince herself that John Brockfield was right. Hereward would be playing somewhere—not with Ivo, but swinging that stupid sword and pretending he was a knight. She made a huge effort to feel righteously angry with him, imagining what she would say to him when she found him to make him know how needlessly worried everyone had been, but all the time she was struggling not to burst into tears.

She came to a place where the bracken beside the path was roughly broken down, as if someone had plunged into the undergrowth there. Nervously she took a few steps into the woodland, but she could see nothing except grey tree-trunks blurred by the softly falling snow.

115

'Hereward!' she called, but there was no reply.

The trail of stamping feet was clear in front of her, winding around the trees. Setting one foot carefully in front of the other, Gwyneth followed it. The track vanished behind a bramble thicket; she skirted it, pulling her cloak away from tendrils that snagged the cloth as she walked.

Then she came to a halt. There was a wide swathe of trampled grass in front of her, beginning to fill up with snow. Some of the brambles had been crushed, too.

'Someone fell . . .' she murmured. 'Or there was a struggle.'

She took a few steps forward, scanning the ground for any signs that would tell her more. Her gaze fell on a worn ankle boot of scuffed brown leather, almost buried in snow; she stared for a moment, hardly realizing what it was. Then she swooped on it and caught it up. It was Hereward's.

'He was here,' Gwyneth whispered, the act of thinking out loud the only thing keeping her from falling to the ground in horror. 'Someone caught him . . . but they didn't kill him, or his body would be here. They must have taken him away, but his shoe fell off.'

With a chill like ice inside her, she remembered what Hereward had told her that morning. She could no longer be sure that the men he had seen were really mummers—not now that Bryan was dead, and Hereward a prisoner. Perhaps he really had found the traitors' camp!

I must find Master Thorson, she decided.

Clutching the boot to her she began hurrying back to the path, only to stop dead with a shriek of alarm when a figure stepped out from behind a tree. Then she relaxed, shaking and struggling to keep back hysterical laughter.

'Ursus, it's you!'

The hermit looked gravely down at her. 'You have heard of the evil deed to the ferryman done this day, Gwyneth?' he said. 'You should not be abroad alone.'

'I was looking for Hereward,' Gwyneth explained. The laughter had died away and she was threatened by tears once again. She held out the boot. 'I found this.' She pointed towards the thicket where the snow was rapidly obliterating the signs of the struggle.

Ursus scanned the place carefully and turned

back to her. 'You think your brother has been taken prisoner?'

'I don't know what to think. But mother sent him on an errand to Master Brockfield this morning, and no one has seen him since. I thought he'd just gone to play, until I found the boot.'

Ursus looked graver still, his blue eyes staring unseeingly into the distance. 'Your brother is not one to play while there are errands to be done.'

'He used not to be,' Gwyneth agreed, 'but he hasn't been the same since he found that stupid sword. He wants to be by himself all the time, and he doesn't tell me anything.' Guiltily she remembered how she had laughed at Hereward when he had come to tell her about the traitors' camp, and shook her head to clear away the tears that welled behind her eyes.

'A sword?' Ursus frowned. 'Tell me about it.'

'He found it in Master Brockfield's field when we were cleaning out his pig shelter. It was buried in the mud of the old lake-bed.'

For an instant, Ursus froze. When he turned his head towards her, his eyes were blue flames. 'I should have known,' he murmured, half to himself. More loudly, he asked, 'Does the sword have a dragon on the hilt in a circle of thorns? Can it cut through anything, even the hardest steel?'

Gwyneth was bewildered. Why was Ursus so concerned about the sword, when all that mattered was finding Hereward? 'There is a dragon,' she replied uncertainly. 'I don't know how well it cuts, though. Hereward will hardly let me touch it.'

Before she had finished speaking, Ursus was heading back towards the path, glancing back to utter the one word, 'Come.'

Gwyneth followed; he was striding so fast that she almost had to run to keep up. 'What's the matter?' she gasped. 'Where are we going? Why is the sword important?'

Ursus did not reply. Gwyneth panted after him until they reached the village, silent now under the falling snow. Only one figure was walking along the street: a tall, black-habited monk, heading for the abbey.

'Brother Timothy!' Ursus called.

He quickened his pace still more, and came up with the monk in the shelter of the abbey gateway. Gwyneth saw Brother Timothy bow his head with the deepest respect, and heard him say, 'How may I serve you?'

'I know not,' Ursus replied. 'Yet serve we must, for a time of great testing is upon us. Traitors have come to Glastonbury, and Excalibur has been found.'

Chapter Nine

'Excalibur!' Gwyneth echoed. 'What do you mean?'

Both men turned to look at her. Their faces were kind, yet she felt that somehow she was not part of the bond that existed between them.

'Excalibur is the sword of King Arthur,' Ursus told her. 'It came from a lake, forged below water, and when Arthur made his last journey to the Isle of Avalon, to a lake it was returned. I fear this is the sword that Hereward has found. The time is not yet for it to reappear in the world, for it brings with it great danger.'

'What danger?' Gwyneth's throat was dry and her voice rasped painfully in her throat. She had heard of the sword Excalibur among the stories of Avalon, of course, but not that it could do any harm. 'Will it hurt Hereward?'

'I think not,' said Brother Timothy. 'It is

dangerous to all but its rightful owner, but there is no evil ambition in your brother, and so he may be safe. Yet in the hands of a wicked man it could do great harm. The man who wields Excalibur has the right to claim the throne of England.'

Gwyneth clapped a hand to her mouth as she realized that once more one of King Arthur's relics had appeared to drag her and everything she held dear into a realm of dark mystery. 'Henry of Truro!' she gasped, and she went on, fighting back panic, 'The traitors have taken Hereward. If he had the sword . . . oh, we must tell Master Thorson at once.'

'A moment.' Ursus took her hands in his and held them firmly as Gwyneth struggled to free herself. 'Did your brother have the sword with him when he left the Crown?'

Gwyneth shook her head. 'I don't know. I didn't see him go.'

'I think that he did not,' the hermit said reflectively. 'For if he had, the traitors would have killed him and left him lying where you found his boot. Gwyneth, is it possible that the traitors have learnt that your brother has Excalibur in his possession?'

'I can't think how . . .' Realization struck Gwyneth like a blow. 'Men broke into the Crown last night! They were searching in our bedroom. They must have been some of the traitors, looking for Excalibur.'

Ursus and Brother Timothy exchanged a swift glance.

'Then they have somehow discovered that Hereward holds Excalibur,' said the hermit. 'They will keep him safe until he tells them where to find it.'

'They might *torture* him.' Gwyneth choked out the words.

'Perhaps,' Brother Timothy said sombrely. 'Or perhaps they will try to deceive him with fair words.'

'In either case,' Ursus went on, 'we must not tell Master Thorson and provoke a hue and cry. That would lead them to kill him, without question.'

Gwyneth stared up at him, blinking back tears. 'Then what can we do?'

'We must go quietly to their camp,' the hermit explained, 'and free Hereward by stealth.'

'But we don't know where it is!' Gwyneth's

tears spilled over and she buried her face in her hands. If she had only listened to Hereward that morning, instead of mocking him, he might have told her exactly where the traitors' camp was located. Instead, she had thought she was being so clever, believing that all he had seen was a band of mummers.

Strong arms went round her and she felt herself being hugged against the rough wool of Brother Timothy's habit.

'Gwyneth.' It was Ursus who spoke, as the monk released her. 'Well do I know your courage. You will need it now. Will you place yourself at my command, to do as I think best? I swear to you by God and his holy saints that I will do all I can to restore your brother to you safely. But we have to take thought for the whole of this land, not just for Hereward. We must make certain that these evil men do not find Excalibur.'

The hermit's blue eyes gazed compellingly into hers. Gwyneth felt the force of his will beating down her own, demanding her trust.

'What if there's a choice?' she whispered. 'Between saving Excalibur and saving Hereward?'

'Please God it will not come to that,' Brother Timothy said.

'Gwyneth, this is Hereward's best chance,' Ursus assured her. 'In saving Excalibur, we will save him too.'

'Then . . . then I'll do as you say.'

'Good.' Ursus's smile blazed at her. 'First we must make certain that Hereward did not have Excalibur with him. Who would know, do you think?'

'My mother sent him out—oh!' Gwyneth ended with a gasp. 'What am I going to tell mother and father?'

'By my advice, not the truth,' Brother Timothy said swiftly. 'If they learn that Hereward is taken by the traitors, nothing will stop them from calling on Master Thorson. And for Hereward's safety, as well as the secrecy of Excalibur, they must not do that.'

Gwyneth was shocked to hear a holy brother advising her to lie to her parents. But the need to save Hereward and Excalibur was so urgent that she realized he was right.

'Can you think of something to tell them?' Ursus asked. 'To keep them from being anxious for a day? That will give us all the time we need to find Hereward.'

Panic blanked out Gwyneth's mind for a moment, and then she nodded.

'Excellent.' Ursus squeezed her shoulder, and she felt strength flow into her, a warmth that not even the thickly falling snow could quench. 'Go then, and find out what you may. I will wait here until you bring me word.'

When Gwyneth entered the kitchen her mother was standing by the fire, stirring a pot. The savoury smell of bean soup filled the kitchen, and Gwyneth wished with all her heart that she could busy herself about her household tasks, and that she had never heard of Excalibur.

'There you are, Gwyneth!' Idony turned at the sound of the door closing. 'Goodness, you're soaked from all that snow. Come here to the fire.'

Gwyneth hung her cloak behind the door and went over to her mother.

'There, stir that a moment,' said Idony, pushing a spoon into her hand, while she went to the kitchen table and began chopping onions. 'Have you found Hereward?'

Gwyneth cleared her throat; it was hard to get the lie out, let alone speak without bursting into tears and rushing to her mother for comfort. 'No, but I know where he is. Master Brockfield told me that he . . . he met Master Short and helped him carry some reeds back to his hut. With the snow so heavy, I expect he'll stay there tonight.'

'Best if he does,' Idony agreed, sounding quite unworried. 'Sim Short's hut is a good step away.'

Staring down at the stirring spoon, Gwyneth tried not to wonder what Sim Short the basket-maker would say if Idony ever thanked him for giving a night's hospitality to Hereward. She did not look at her mother as she asked, 'Was Hereward carrying anything when he left?'

'No.' From behind Gwyneth the sound of rhythmic chopping stopped. 'What a question! Why do you want to know?'

'I . . . I couldn't find my comb,' Gwyneth explained falteringly. Relief made her knees buckle as she realized that Hereward did not have Excalibur with him, which meant that the

127

sword was safe from the traitors' hands—for now. 'I thought Hereward might have taken it for a jest.'

Idony clicked her tongue. 'If I know you, young mistress, you haven't looked properly. Don't blame Hereward for your carelessness, even if you have quarrelled with him.'

Gwyneth muttered an apology. Idony brought the onions to the fire and dropped them into the pot of soup. 'There, that just needs to simmer,' she said, taking back the spoon from Gwyneth. Smiling to show that her brief annoyance was over, she suggested, 'Why don't you go and change out of that wet gown, and then have a good look for your comb? I shan't need you to help here until supper is ready.'

Gwyneth agreed and escaped from the kitchen, knowing that Ursus and Brother Timothy would be waiting for her. She paused in the passage, wondering where she ought to start looking for Excalibur. She was sure the sword was not in their bedroom. The traitors had not found it there, and besides, Hereward was so possessive about his discovery that he would never have put it where she could easily find it. That meant she had all of the inn, the yard, the garden, and the outbuildings to search—and every moment that slipped away brought Hereward closer to torture and death.

While she was hesitating the door opened and Ivo Thorson stepped into the passage, shaking snow off his cloak. Gwyneth bit back a groan. The last thing she wanted now was Ivo and his jesting.

But Ivo had not come to play tricks. 'Gwyneth, where's your father?' he asked. 'I've a message for him.'

'I haven't seen him,' Gwyneth replied, 'but he's usually in the taproom at this hour.'

Ivo thanked her. 'Father is trying to find the man who killed Bryan,' he told Gwyneth, which explained his unusual seriousness. 'He wants to ask your father if there are any guests here that he can't account for.'

'All our guests are pilgrims, I think,' said Gwyneth. She was beginning to suspect that Bryan's death must somehow be connected with the band of traitors, since it had happened not far from the place where Hereward had been seized, but that was something else she couldn't tell Ivo or the sheriff.

Ivo was pushing open the taproom door when an idea struck her. 'Ivo, do you know where Hereward might be likely to hide something?'

Glancing back, Ivo shook his head. 'Why do you want to know?'

'I think he took my comb.' Gwyneth seized on the excuse that had served for her mother. 'I can't find it, and now he's gone off with Master Short, so I can't ask him what he did with it.'

Ivo shrugged as if a missing comb didn't interest him, and was turning away again when he suddenly stopped. 'Wait—now I remember. Back in the summer, Hereward and I used to hide things in the thatch above the well in the yard. He might have put it there. I'll show you if you want.'

'No, Ivo, I can do it,' Gwyneth said hastily. 'And thank you.'

She waited until her friend had disappeared into the taproom before plunging out into the yard again. Stumbling through the powdery snow, glancing nervously around in case someone spotted her, she reached out with shaking, frozen fingers and peeled back the edge of the thatch above the well. Lying on the wooden framework below was a scrap of canvas holding a couple of slingstones and two pieces of wood lashed together and roughly shaped into a dagger. Thrust further into the shadows was a long, narrow bundle wrapped up in sacking.

'Excalibur!' she breathed.

Fumbling to get a grip on it in hands stiff with cold, she hurried across the yard and out through the archway, thankful that the windows were shuttered and no one was likely to see her dashing off without her cloak. The winter daylight was already dying; the market-place was deserted and the street empty. All the villagers would be indoors, building up their fires and barring doors and windows against the cold.

Ursus and Brother Timothy were waiting in the shelter of the abbey gateway.

'You have news?' asked the hermit, stepping forward. He halted in surprise when Gwyneth held out the bundle to him.

'More than news,' she declared breathlessly.

Without taking the bundle from her, Ursus laid one hand on it, and even in the twilight she was aware of the intensity in his blue eyes. 'Truly you have done well,' he said.

His praise was like a fire glowing inside Gwyneth, but she could not let herself enjoy it. 'Can we go to find Hereward now?' she begged.

'Not yet.' It was Brother Timothy who replied. As she began to protest, he added, 'Think, Gwyneth. Already it grows dark, and we do not know where the traitors' camp may be. What use to blunder about the woods all night?'

Ursus nodded. 'He is right, Gwyneth. We will leave tomorrow at dawn. Do not fear. The traitors will do nothing to Hereward tonight.'

Gwyneth wondered how he could be so sure, but there was no point in arguing. 'Will you take the sword with you?' she asked.

'No.' Ursus lifted his hand off the sackcloth and stepped back, leaving her to hold the bundle. 'If the traitors have already searched your room, they will not expect to find it there. Guard it well until the morning.'

Raising a hand in farewell, he stepped out from under the archway and vanished into the whirling snow.

★ ★ ★

That night, before she blew out her taper, Gwyneth unfolded the sacking and looked down at the sword. Someone had cleaned up the blade since her brother rescued it from the mud. It gleamed like water in the quivering light of the taper. But the hilt was still rusty, the coiled dragon hardly distinguishable. It scarcely looked like the Excalibur Gwyneth had heard about in old tales, the fabled sword of King Arthur. She found it hard to believe that it held the key to England's destiny; it certainly was not worth her brother's life.

'Dear God, keep Hereward safe,' she prayed as she wrapped the sword in the sacking once more, and put out the light.

Chapter Ten

Hereward's head swam, and he thought he was going to be sick. An evil-smelling sack covered him as far as his waist and cords were bound around his chest, pinning his arms to his sides. More cords lashed his ankles together; Hereward remembered how satisfying it had been to land a few good kicks on his assailants before they had managed to bind him.

That satisfaction was wearing thin now. Once he was tied up, they had slung him across the back of a mule and set off through the forest. Hereward guessed that they were on their way to the traitors' camp. Part of the mule's saddle was digging into his stomach and his head lolled, jolted by the animal's uneven gait over the roots and hollows of the forest path.

When he could think of anything except his discomfort, he tried to work out why they had taken him. He had watched Galfridas Hood murder Bryan the ferryman, which was reason enough for the Hoodman to want him dead. Capturing him instead, carrying him back to the camp, made no sense at all.

He was beginning to drift into a nauseous, uneasy sleep when he heard the sound of voices. A moment later the mule halted. Hereward was hauled off its back and the cords around his ankles were slashed so he could stand on his feet. As he staggered to keep his balance someone grabbed him, untied his arms, and pulled the sack from his head.

Blinking, Hereward looked around him. As he had guessed, they had brought him back to the traitors' camp. It was almost dark under the trees, though he did not think that much time had passed since he was taken prisoner. He shivered in the raw cold and hoped the traitors would not think he was trembling with fear.

Galfridas Hood was standing in front of him, pointing his sword at Hereward's chest. Osbert Teller stood beside him, the sack bundled in his arms and an unpleasant grin on his face.

'Well, Master Mason,' Galfridas Hood said

softly. 'Be welcome to our camp. Do as you're bid, and you will come to no harm.'

Hereward did not believe the man's reassurance for one moment, but he tried to speak bravely. 'What do you want with me?'

'All in good time,' said the Hoodman. 'I have other business just now. There is no escape from here, and none of your friends knows where to find you. Your only chance is to co-operate with me.'

'Never!' Hereward retorted. 'You're a traitor and a murderer.'

An ugly look flashed into Galfridas Hood's mismatched eyes. 'You'll sing another tune shortly,' he promised. 'Osbert, take him to your tent. If he causes trouble, it will be the worse for you.'

Osbert ducked his head, and as the Hoodman strode away he grabbed Hereward by the front of his tunic. 'You heard him,' he growled. 'Give me any trouble and you'll regret it.' He shoved Hereward away from him. 'Now move.'

'I want to use the privy,' Hereward demanded, meeting the dwarf's eyes with a defiant stare. He was beginning to recover his senses now, and he had remembered the ill-smelling trench on the edge of the camp. If he could get as far as that, maybe he could escape after all.

'All right.' Osbert jerked his head in the direction of the trench. 'But don't think I can't see what's in your head. There are archers on guard all round the camp, and they'd put a shaft into your back without thinking twice.'

Hereward believed him. They passed one of them, a desperate-looking man with a longbow in his hands, and a quiver of arrows slung over one shoulder. His gaze flicked coldly over Hereward, who wondered if he was one of the traitors who had escaped hanging in Bristol.

Relieving himself in the trench, Hereward did not dare to make a move. If he tried to flee, Osbert Teller would raise the alarm and he would be dead for certain, with no chance of telling what he knew. He would have to obey his captors for the time being and hope for a better opportunity to escape.

Osbert Teller's tent was at the other side of the camp. It was no more than a few ragged pieces of hide stretched over poles; Hereward had to stoop to go inside. A couple of dirty sheepskins were spread on the floor, along with a blanket, and there was a wooden chest near the entrance where Osbert seated himself. The air reeked of sweat and stale food.

Hereward sat cross-legged on the sheepskins and glared up at Osbert Teller, determined not to let him see how frightened he was. 'Just what I'd expect of you,' he jeered, hoping that if he made the dwarf angry he might get careless. 'Working for murderers and traitors!'

Osbert Teller merely grinned at him. 'Say what you like. You'll sing another tune before long.'

He picked up a waterskin which lay beside the chest and took a swig from it. Hereward was desperately thirsty, but the dwarf didn't offer him a drink, and he was too proud to ask for one.

Trying to ignore his captor, he gazed out through the triangular tent opening into the camp, in case an escape route became clear. He had lost track of the hours; the dull winter daylight did not tell him how close the sun was to setting. The fire at the centre of the clearing was still burning, with a few men grouped around it. Closer to the trees, Hereward made out the glow of a second fire, and heard the regular ringing sound of a hammer on metal. Though Hereward could not see him from here, he knew Hywel Smith must be at work. Clearly Hywel had no idea what sort of men he was working for; the gentlest of souls, he would never knowingly help traitors and would be horrified if he found out that Hereward was their prisoner. Hereward wondered if there was any way he could alert Hywel so they could try to escape together, but it would take far too long to explain to the smith who his new masters really were; someone was sure to come upon them before they could get away.

Further round the clearing was the line of tethered horses; Hereward thought wildly of cutting one free and galloping for safety, but he rejected that plan too. It would make too much noise; he would be safer slipping away in silence. Then he noticed that a few white flakes were beginning to fall, and his heart sank. Even if he did manage to escape from the camp, the traitors would be able to track him easily with snow on the ground.

Osbert Teller had taken a knife from his belt

and was twirling it in his stubby fingers. He grinned nastily as he watched Hereward. 'That's right,' he said. 'You sit nice and quiet, and there won't be any trouble. You're not going anywhere.'

Hereward ignored him at first, until he realized that it might be good to keep the dwarf talking. 'What are you doing here?' he asked. 'I thought you were working for Master Kharab.'

Osbert gave a disagreeable snort. 'That heathen! I worked for him for a while—I've got to eat, haven't I?—but I never meant to stop with him. He treated me like a slave.'

You mean he expected you to do some work, Hereward translated silently. 'Galfridas Hood doesn't treat you any better,' he pointed out.

The dwarf's eyes flashed angrily. 'You keep your nose out of my affairs,' he growled. 'And don't say nothing bad about the Hoodman, or you might find yourself short of a tongue.'

Hereward suppressed a shiver; he could believe that all too easily. 'Where did you meet him?'

'He had business with Master Kharab,' Osbert Teller replied. The dwarf's voice grew boastful. 'He could see I'd be useful to him. I know all the paths round here, see, through the woods and the marshes. And I know folk in the village. I can tell the Hoodman who'd be willing to join his army.'

'But they're traitors!' Hereward exclaimed. 'Doesn't that mean anything to you?'

Master Teller made a contemptuous noise. 'Traitors to Richard, maybe—but Richard is no true king. Henry of Truro will be a better lord to me. When he holds power, I'll be rich.' He stuck his thumbs in his belt and gave Hereward a wide, satisfied smile.

'And you really believe that?' said Hereward. 'Have you even met Henry of Truro? If I were you I'd not trust any promises the Hoodman made to me.'

Osbert Teller's smile vanished in a snarl of anger. He jumped up and aimed a kick at Hereward, who rolled away from it towards the side of the tent. The dwarf grabbed him by the neck of his tunic and threw him down on top of the sheepskins.

'Shut your mouth!' he snarled. 'Think you're so clever, don't you? We'll see how clever you feel when the Hoodman comes back.'

Hereward felt dread gnawing at his stomach

like a worm. For a short while his hopes of escape and his curiosity about Osbert Teller had helped him forget what the Hoodman had in store for him. The one question he could not answer was what the man wanted with him. What did he have that could possibly help the traitors?

He was just wondering if he could get any information out of Master Teller when there was a footstep outside the tent and Galfridas Hood himself ducked inside. Snow glittered on his shoulders and his hair, no colder than the glitter in his eyes. Too tall to stand upright under the sagging tent roof, he squatted in front of Hereward, who sat up to face him, willing himself not to tremble.

'Master Mason.' The Hoodman's voice was soft; Hereward would have been less terrified if he had shouted. 'At last I have leisure to attend to you.'

'What do you want?' Hereward's voice shook in spite of all his efforts to keep it steady.

'The answers to a few questions.'

'I won't tell you anything!'

Galfridas Hood smiled—an oddly gentle smile

that froze Hereward's heart. 'I think you will, if you know what's good for you.'

'And then you'll let me go? You must be mad if you think I'll believe that!'

'Of course not. You know I cannot let you go. You have seen too much. But later—when my plans have borne fruit—then I might release you, if you don't give me any trouble.'

Hereward's eyes narrowed as he tried to size the man up. He might even be telling the truth. If his plan to seize the throne succeeded, there would be no harm that Hereward, a mere boy, could do to him. Best to pretend he believed him, at least, and gain some time.

'What do you want to know?' he asked.

'Very sensible.' Galfridas Hood's eyes glinted with satisfaction. 'Tell me this—where did you find the sword?'

Hereward stared at him, genuinely astonished, and lost the chance to pretend that he had no idea what the man was talking about. 'How do you know about that?' he gasped.

'Never mind.' The Hoodman's hand rapped impatiently on the ground. 'Where did you find it?'

'In the field where Master Brockfield keeps his pigs,' Hereward answered, seeing no reason to lie. 'It was buried in the old lake-bed.'

For some reason the reply seemed to please Master Hood. His smile broadened, and the gleam in his eyes was pure greed. His voice was taut with urgency as he asked, 'Where is it now?'

This was the time to lie, Hereward realized. He had no idea why the sword was important to Galfridas Hood, but the look in his eyes alone was good reason to make sure he never found it. 'I threw it away.'

'What?' Anger replaced the pleasure in the Hoodman's face. 'I don't believe you.'

Hereward shrugged, trying to look unconcerned. 'It was only an old, rusty thing. I threw it away.'

'Where?'

'I don't know. Somewhere in the woods.'

The Hoodman leant forward and gripped Hereward by the shoulders, his fingers digging in cruelly. 'Could you take me to the place?'

'No, I don't think so.' Hereward looked into his eyes, daunted by the menace he saw there. 'I don't remember.'

Galfridas Hood released him and lashed one hand across his face. Hereward rocked with the force of the blow, and felt the salt taste of blood in his mouth.

'You're lying,' snarled the Hoodman. 'No one could hold that sword and then cast it away. Tell me where it really is.'

'I've told you.' Hereward shrank away from him. There was no point in hiding his fear now; let the man think he was too terrified to lie. 'I don't know where it is.'

Gripping Hereward by the shoulder, the Hoodman slid a knife from his belt and held it so that the point glittered close to Hereward's eyes. 'I could blind you.' His voice was perfectly calm, as if the monstrous threat was common-place for him. 'Or I could cut out your tongue. Now tell me the truth.'

Hereward forced his head back, away from the sharp blade. 'No—please, don't—I don't know any more.'

Terror surged through him as he waited for the knife to plunge into his eye. Instead, at that very moment a shout came from outside the tent. 'Master Hood! Are you in there?'

'What is it?' the Hoodman called back, not taking his gaze from Hereward's face.

'A messenger from my lord Henry, sir.'

The Hoodman let out a curse and flung Hereward back on the sheepskins. 'Don't think we've finished,' he said. 'I'll be back.' Rising to his feet, he aimed a vicious kick at Hereward's ribs and strode out.

'I told you you'd not feel so clever when the Hoodman had finished with you,' the dwarf sneered at Hereward.

Hereward's vision was blurring. Pain stabbed through his face and ribs, and every muscle in his body ached with exhaustion. He tried to sit up, but black waves surged over him, and, without knowing how, he found that he was lying down again with his face buried in the greasy sheepskins. With a defeated sigh, he let the darkness claim him.

Hereward opened his eyes. He was engulfed in blackness, and for a moment he could not remember where he was. A rhythmic grunting sound came from nearby. His muscles shrieked in protest as he turned his head and saw a faint break in the darkness where the flap in the tent did not quite meet.

Memory flooded back, and with it the sense of his own danger. He could just make out a huddled shape beside him, between him and the tent opening, that he guessed was the sleeping Osbert Teller. The grunting noise was the dwarf's snores.

Hereward's breath came faster as he realized that this was his chance of escape. The camp was quiet; night had fallen and most of the traitors would be sleeping like Osbert. If he could wriggle out under the side of the tent, he stood a chance of slipping away into the trees.

He sat up gingerly, trying to ignore how painful it was to move. He began to slide backwards, still keeping an eye on Osbert, but before he reached the side of the tent he discovered that there was a cord round his wrist, tying his arm to something.

At the same moment the dwarf let out a louder grunt, and his huddled shape floundered upright. There was a vicious tug on Hereward's wrist, and Hereward realized that the other end of the cord was tied round Osbert Teller's arm.

'Restless, are we?' The dwarf leant over Hereward, who could just make out his squashed features and smell the ale on his breath. 'You thought Master Teller was stupid, didn't you? You thought I'd go to sleep and let you get away?'

Hereward had thought just that, and cursed himself for underestimating his enemy.

'Lie down and keep quiet,' the dwarf grunted. 'There's some of us want to sleep.'

For a moment Hereward obeyed, but his fingers were worrying away at the knotted cord; in the darkness he hoped Osbert would not notice that he was trying to free himself.

At first he thought that the dwarf had gone back to sleep, even though the snoring did not start up again. He had just managed to free himself when Master Teller sat up again, letting out a noisy yawn. Hereward just managed to grab the loose end of the cord so that it looked as if it was still tied to his wrist.

Osbert Teller shifted across the tent to grab the waterskin—which Hereward suspected held ale, not water—and took a long drink. Hereward scrambled after him so the dwarf would believe he was still tethered by the cord.

As Master Teller put the stopper back on the skin, Hereward said, 'What's that?'

'What?'

'I heard something, outside. A voice.'

The dwarf gave a bad-tempered grunt. 'I didn't hear nothing.'

'There it is again,' Hereward told him. 'I think it's Master Hood, calling you.'

Osbert hesitated, but, as Hereward had hoped, his fear of the Hoodman was enough for him to make certain that he had not been summoned. He crawled to the tent opening; at once Hereward trapped the cord under the corner of the wooden chest and slid rapidly backwards. The edge of the tent scraped along his back, and then he was out in the open.

With a rapid glance around he dived for the shelter of the nearest bush. His ruse would not deceive Master Teller for more than a moment, and by then he must be well away. Ducking down, he scuttled from one bush to the next until he gained the edge of the trees.

He was limping because at some point in his struggle with his captors he had lost a boot; stooping, he wrenched off the other one and thrust it deep into some thorns, before going on again.

Hereward did not deceive himself that he was safe. There would be guards posted around the camp to keep watch through the night, though he did not know where they were. He could see better now; a faint dawn light reflected off the snow-covered ground, and he realized that the night was almost over. His stomach lurched as he looked behind him and saw his own tracks betraying his escape route.

He was edging along, trying to stay under cover, when he heard the sound he had dreaded: a bellow of rage from the tent he had left, as Osbert Teller discovered the trick with the cord. Hereward couldn't help grinning to think of the trouble the dwarf would be in now.

But his own troubles were too pressing to enjoy the thought for long. Already men were peering out of their tents, wanting to know what the noise was about. The guards would be alerted within a heartbeat. Hereward was just about to launch himself across a gap among the trees when a man stepped into it, his bow at the ready with an arrow on the string. Hereward froze, and as the man swivelled round he was forced to crawl into a hazel thicket, back towards the centre of the camp.

More men were shouting now; in the rising clamour Hereward could not make out individual voices. Someone blundered past him, close enough to reach out and touch, but he never spotted Hereward crouching in the undergrowth. At least, Hereward thought, if they crashed around like that they would soon cover his tracks with their own.

The fracas had forced him back to the edge of the clearing, where he spotted the commanding figure of Galfridas Hood. The fire had been stoked and men were lighting torches at it before hurrying towards the trees, the streaming yellow flames held high above their heads. Fear almost paralysed Hereward as he realized that within a few moments he would surely be discovered.

The tramping of feet heralded the arrival of one of the torchbearers; the light of the flames showed Hereward the blunt features of Clem Ludel the stonemason. Another man was hard on his heels. They stood together not a yard from

Hereward; stealthily he closed his fingers around a stone and lobbed it into the bushes as far as he could.

Master Ludel jumped and raised his torch higher. 'Over there!'

'That?' The other man sounded contemptuous. 'That was a rat.'

'That was no rat.' Clem Ludel set off in the direction of the sound. Over his shoulder he added, 'Do you want to tell the Hoodman you let his prisoner escape?'

At that his companion set off after him and they both vanished into the bushes, with only the glow of the torch through the leaves to tell Hereward where they had gone.

Wriggling along on his stomach behind clumps of bracken, he found himself approaching the other fire. Hywel Smith was lying beside it, bundled in a blanket. Hereward wished he could rouse his friend so they could escape together, but the risk of discovery was too great. In his moment's hesitation the smith sat up and their eyes met. Hywel's face split instantly into a wide grin, and he opened his mouth to call Hereward's name.

Hereward made frantic signs for silence. The smith's grin disappeared; he looked puzzled and began, 'What ails you?'

Just when Hereward felt he would be discovered for sure, a man leading a mule tramped between him and Hywel, giving Hereward the chance to duck back into the undergrowth. He bit back a yell of pain as a thorn drove deep into one stockinged foot. As he crawled rapidly away he heard the smith's bewildered voice behind him: 'Hereward, where have you gone?' Hereward prayed fervently that if the Hoodman heard him he would only think that Hywel was joining in the search.

A moment later he realized that he was approaching the horse lines. The horses were restless, pulling against their tethers as if the noise in the camp had disturbed them. Saddles and bridles were heaped up nearby; as Hereward reached the pile he caught sight of a hunting knife fastened to one of the saddles. He stretched out a hand and drew it from its sheath.

His grip on the hilt was comforting. It did not seem to thrum in his hand like the sword had done, but at least it evened his chances if he came across an armed traitor. And it could have other uses, he thought, turning back to the horses. He could not steal a horse to escape, but they might still help him.

Daring to rise to his feet, he ran along the line of tethered animals, cutting the ropes that held them. Behind him the horses milled around in alarm, breaking out into the clearing or trampling into the trees. Somebody yelled a warning.

Under cover of the added chaos, Hereward risked sprinting across an open space and into the trees beyond. He waited for the shout that would tell him he was discovered, or even for an arrow in his back, but he reached the shelter of the trees unscathed. For a moment he stood panting, bathed in sweat and shaking from relief as he listened to the growing clamour in the camp behind him. Then he turned his back on it and headed for the village as fast as his feet could carry him.

Chapter Eleven

Gwyneth crept stealthily into the inn yard, the sword in its wrappings clutched to her chest, and closed the kitchen door softly behind her. The snow had stopped, but a thick white blanket lay over the cobbles. Grey dawn light showed her the figures of two men: Brother Timothy and Ursus, muffled in cloaks over their habits and each holding the reins of a horse. Picking up her skirt in her free hand, Gwyneth hurried across to join them.

'Is it time? May we go to find Hereward now?'

Ursus simply nodded, but Brother Timothy said, 'There is grave danger ahead of us. Will you not stay here, Gwyneth, and trust us to bring your brother back safely?'

'No!' Gwyneth tightened her grip on the sword hilt. 'Please don't leave me behind.'

Ursus put a hand reassuringly on the young

monk's shoulder. 'Peace, Brother. My heart tells me that Gwyneth has a part to play in this before all is done.'

Brother Timothy did not protest any more, though his bony face was troubled as he climbed into the saddle of his horse, a solid black gelding from the abbey stables. Gwyneth tucked the sword into her girdle and scrambled up behind him, locking her arms around his waist. As she did so she caught sight of a gleam of steel among the folds of his black habit, and realized that her friend—the monk, the man of peace—was also bearing a sword.

Ursus swung himself into the saddle of a chestnut mare. In the midst of her anxiety Gwyneth could not help but feel surprised that a hermit should be so easy with horses, as if he had been riding all his life. His face was intent and his blue eyes shone with determination. 'Let us ride,' he said.

Snow muffled the sound of the horses' hooves as they walked underneath the arch and along the street. The bell for lauds had not rung, and Gwyneth expected their departure to be unseen, but as they approached the abbey they heard the jingle of a bridle and two other horsemen appeared through the archway.

Gwyneth's heart beat faster as she recognized them: Finn Thorson, and Godfrey de Massard on his superb black stallion. Both men's faces were grimly set and Gwyneth was terrified that the sheriff would want to know their business; he might even try to stop them.

'Good morrow.' Master Thorson reined in his horse, guiding it across their path so that Ursus and Brother Timothy had no choice but to stop. 'You're out early, gentlemen.'

Ursus ignored the question in his voice, merely bowing his head. 'And so are you, Master Sheriff.'

Finn Thorson gave him a curious glance. Gwyneth was astonished to realize that she had never seen Ursus among the villagers until now. Though Ivo and Amabel had once almost come upon him, when she and Hereward met him he had always been alone, and the only other person to speak with him had been Brother Timothy. Somehow she felt that this was a moment of immense importance, like the crossing of a great river, though she did not understand why.

'We have word of the escaped prisoners,' Finn

Thorson explained. 'Last night Margery Carver came upon one of them filching a chicken from her pen, and raised the alarm. We caught him, God be praised, and at last he told us where to find the rest of them.'

'Master Thorson and I are raising a party to raid their camp,' Father Godfrey added.

'You *know* where to find the traitors' camp?' Gwyneth could not keep back the exclamation.

'Yes—and you cannot come with us, Gwyneth,' Finn Thorson said. 'Get you home to your parents.'

'No!' Gwyneth protested, clinging more tightly to Brother Timothy's waist. 'They've taken Hereward prisoner!'

'What?' The sheriff's face darkened. 'Why was I not told?'

'I—I've only just found out,' Gwyneth said wildly, praying that God would forgive her for all the lies she was being forced to tell. 'Master Thorson, you mustn't raid the camp. If you do, they'll kill Hereward.'

Finn Thorson was silent, his eyes clouded with concern.

'Let us ride ahead,' Ursus suggested. 'We'll

enter the camp by stealth and free the boy. When he is safe you may mount your raid.'

By the time he finished speaking his tone had become commanding, and to Gwyneth's surprise the sheriff agreed as willingly as if some great lord had given him an order.

'Very well. I will follow you with as many men as I can gather.'

'Then where is the camp?' Brother Timothy asked.

'I know,' said Father Godfrey. If he was surprised that a monk and a hermit should be mounted and willing to ride into battle, he did not show it. 'I'll ride with you and guide you.'

'Good.' Ursus's warm blue gaze rested on the priest and Gwyneth was even more surprised to see Father Godfrey flush, as if the praise embarrassed him. She had hardly ever known him lose his air of aristocratic arrogance.

The black-robed priest turned his horse and led the way down the village street towards the woods. Finn Thorson went the other way, into the village to rouse more men.

The dawn light was strengthening as the horsemen left the last houses of the village behind and urged their mounts into a trot. Bouncing around behind Brother Timothy, Gwyneth found their pace frustratingly slow, though she knew horses could not gallop safely along these narrow paths with snow underfoot. She was desperate to reach the camp and find Hereward before the traitors tortured him into telling where they could find Excalibur.

Father Godfrey led them deep into the forest, along twisting paths where the horses had to slow to a walk again. Gwyneth hoped he knew where he was going; the thought struck her like an arrow through the heart that the captured traitor might have lied about where the camp lay, to save his companions.

At last the priest reined in his horse and slid from the saddle. 'The camp should be close by,' he said in a low voice. 'We should go on foot from here.'

Brother Timothy dismounted and lifted Gwyneth down. He and Ursus tethered their horses; Father Godfrey pushed his stallion's reins into Gwyneth's hands. 'Stay here,' he ordered. 'Keep watch for Master Thorson and his men.'

Gwyneth opened her mouth to protest, but

the priest had already turned away, following Ursus and Brother Timothy through the trees. Gwyneth shot a furious glare at his retreating back, then tethered the stallion to a tree branch beside the other horses, and set out cautiously after the three men. She had no intention of staying where she was, not when her brother's life was in danger.

She had not crept forward many paces when she heard movement from ahead, and the sound of voices. Brother Timothy checked, said something to Ursus, and went on. Gwyneth's breath came faster and her heart pounded as she realized they were approaching the edge of the camp.

Then a shout echoed from somewhere above their heads, answered a moment later by other shouts from further off. Gwyneth froze. The traitors had posted lookouts and they had been spotted!

Brother Timothy and Ursus exchanged a glance, and Gwyneth heard the hermit say, 'We must go on.'

There was a silken sound as Brother Timothy drew his sword. Father Godfrey was armed, too; both men hurried forward, no longer trying to conceal themselves. Ursus glanced back as if he had known that Gwyneth would be there, and beckoned to her.

'We'll search for your brother,' he murmured. 'You go that way.'

Gwyneth realized that they were standing on the edge of a clearing. Somewhere ahead was the red glow of a fire. Tents encircled it, along with one or two rough wooden huts. As she stared, three or four men appeared, running towards Brother Timothy and Father Godfrey. Their swords clashed; for a moment Gwyneth froze as she saw how terribly her friends were outnumbered, with more men running up from the centre of the camp. But the priest and the monk lacked no courage as they raised their swords to defend themselves. Father Godfrey fought with all the skill of a trained knight, and Gwyneth was amazed to see that Brother Timothy could handle himself just as efficiently. Father Godfrey leapt forward, his habit flapping like a raven's wings as he swung his sword. Brother Timothy parried a blow from the first of his attackers and whirled smoothly to beat the weapon out of the hand of a second. *Where had a village boy learned to use a sword like that?* Gwyneth wondered in a daze.

'Gwyneth!' Ursus's voice brought her back to the danger she was in. 'Search, while they're distracted.'

Gwyneth hurried off in the direction he was pointing. Coming to the first tent, she lifted the flap, but there was nothing inside except for tumbled blankets and a wooden trencher with a few scraps of bread on it. She straightened up, gazing round desperately, trying to ignore the clamour where Brother Timothy and Father Godfrey were fighting for their lives.

'Hereward! Hereward!' she shouted.

If her brother could hear her above the noise of the fighting, he did not respond. Gwyneth dashed to the first of the wooden huts. Wrenching the door open, she halted in amazement with her brother's name dying on her lips. At the far end of the hut, seated on a sack of grain, was Marion le Fevre.

'Gwyneth!' The embroideress jumped to her feet and flew towards Gwyneth, her hands held out. 'Oh, Gwyneth, I've been so frightened!'

Her lustrous black hair was tangled and her face white, streaked with tears. When Gwyneth grasped her hands she could feel her trembling.

'Mistress le Fevre!' she exclaimed. 'What are you doing here?'

Marion bent her head, beginning to sob. 'I came here yesterday with one of the men . . . the mummers. At least, I thought they were mummers. The surcoats were finished, and I wanted to fit them on, to make sure they needed no extra stitching. But when I got here, they took the surcoats from me and put me in this foul hut. They threatened to kill me if I set one foot outside. I've been here all night . . . I thought no one would come!'

'Well, I'm here now,' Gwyneth said soothingly, putting an arm around her. 'Come with me, and you'll soon be safe.'

The embroideress looked at her with green, tear-filled eyes. 'Gwyneth, you're so brave!'

'Just come.' Gwyneth urged her gently towards the door. 'I've got to look for Hereward.'

'No, no.' Marion le Fevre's hands tightened on Gwyneth's. 'Don't leave me alone—oh!'

The last word was a gasp. Before she and

Gwyneth could set foot outside the hut, a man's figure darkened the doorway. Gwyneth froze. It was Galfridas Hood, and in his hand he held a drawn sword.

Chapter Twelve

Hereward darted through the forest from one clump of bushes to the next, until the traitors' camp was far behind him. He was beginning to breathe more easily, certain now that he had escaped with his life. He felt exhausted, and the pain from the beating Galfridas Hood had given him made his legs stiff and clumsy, but he kept going. He had to take word to Finn Thorson so that the sheriff could come and arrest the traitors before they carried out their plot to put Henry of Truro on the throne.

He slowed down as his stockinged feet grew sore from the hard ground, but he had reached more familiar territory when he heard the sound of men and horses moving through the trees. His heart gave a huge thump as he wondered if the traitors were pursuing him after all. Then he realized that the newcomers were approaching from the direction of the village, not the camp.

Still cautious, he crept forward until he was looking out at a forest path from the shelter of a gorse bush. The advancing men were still out of sight. Hereward was crouching down into cover, from where he could see them unobserved, when someone grabbed him from behind.

'Spying, are you?' a voice hissed in his ear.

Hereward tried to leap up, but his captor wrenched one of his arms behind him and pushed him forward through the undergrowth as far as the path. Hereward twisted round, trying to see his face, but the man was hooded, and in the dim light of dawn Hereward could not make out his features.

'I'm not a spy!' he protested angrily. 'Let me go!'

His captor laughed. Gripping the hilt of the hunting knife that Hereward had thrust into his belt, he pulled it out and tossed it into the bushes. 'Let you go?' he said. 'You must think I was born yesterday.'

The noise grew louder and armed horsemen appeared round the turn of the path. Hereward's captor shook him roughly and growled, 'Let's see what you've got to say for yourself, shall we?'

For answer, Hereward let out a shout of relief. Now that he could see the approaching men clearly, he recognized Finn Thorson in the lead, followed by a group of his own men and some of the Glastonbury villagers, mounted or on foot. Hereward spotted Tom Smith, a heavy hammer clutched in his huge fists, his Uncle Owen and Matt Green, with more of the stonemasons, and Dickon Carver brandishing a reaping hook.

'What's going on?' Master Thorson reined in his chestnut cob and looked down. 'Is that Hereward?'

'What?' Hereward's captor released him suddenly. Hereward spun round to see him pushing back his hood, revealing himself to be one of Finn Thorson's men. 'Well, so it is. I'm sorry, lad,' he said sheepishly. 'I couldn't see you properly back there in the bushes.'

Hereward had no time to waste on him. 'Master Thorson,' he began, turning back to the sheriff. 'You must come with me at once. The traitors—'

'We know,' Finn Thorson said tersely. 'We caught one of them last night and he told us

168

where to find their camp. Gwyneth thought you were a prisoner there.'

'I was, but I escaped. Is Gwyneth with you?' Hereward asked, peering through the half-light to see if his sister was among the villagers.

'No, she went on ahead with Brother Timothy and Father Godfrey, and some hermit—'

'Ursus?' Briefly Hereward was reassured to think that Gwyneth was with their friend, until he remembered how many men Galfridas Hood had at his command. 'We have to stop them!' he exclaimed. 'They'll be outnumbered . . . they'll be killed or captured, and I'm not even there!'

'We'll do our best,' said the sheriff. 'We can't be far behind them. You get home safe, lad, and we'll look after Gwyneth, don't you worry.'

'But I can't just leave her!' Hereward protested.

The sheriff did not hear him. He had already set spurs to his horse, and the rest of his troop streamed past Hereward, the villagers on foot bringing up the rear. Hereward's mouth set with determination. He waited until the last man had passed, then joined them, limping along at the rear. Tom Smith, who was just in front of him, glanced back; Hereward braced himself for an argument, but the smith only nodded grimly as if he approved of Hereward's courage.

His feet thudded on the ground, each step jolting right through his body, and every bone and muscle ached with exhaustion. Hereward wanted nothing more than to lie down and sleep right there in the cold, snow-filled woods, but he refused to let himself stop. His quarrel with Gwyneth could not have seemed less important, and now that she needed help, Hereward meant to be there to rescue her, or die trying.

As Galfridas Hood stepped into the hut, Marion le Fevre let out a little moaning cry and covered her face with her hands. Gwyneth moved protectively in front of her to face the swordsman. Hereward had been right; this was the Hoodman, who was to lead Henry of Truro's army. Icy snow-melt seemed to creep through all her body as he smiled.

'Gwyneth Mason,' he said. 'What brings you here? And what do you think your parents will give me to let you go?'

'Traitor!' Gwyneth spat.

'Say as you please, girl.' The Hoodman seemed unmoved by her accusation. 'It will do you no good.'

'And what good will it do you, to put Henry of Truro on the throne?' Gwyneth retorted. 'He's a traitor too—do you think he will keep faith with you?'

She had hoped to distract him, so that she might dart out through the door with Marion, but the cold, mismatched eyes never left her face.

'Henry of Truro?' he sneered. 'That fool. Once I served him, but no longer. Now I shall claim the throne for myself. I know of something that is even more powerful than the blood he claims to share with Richard. And you, girl, shall help me find it.'

'I don't know what you mean.' Gwyneth's voice shook, and she hoped the Hoodman would think it was only fear. She knew very well what he meant, and if he realized that the sacking-wrapped bundle which she wore thrust through her girdle was the fabled sword Excalibur, her life would be worth nothing. Hood's loyalty to Henry of Truro had crumbled to dust before the lure of the sword and the power it could give. He would kill her and take it, and the whole of England would be his to pillage and oppress. When he fought off the intruders who had broken into the inn to look for the sword, he must have been pretending, to avoid any suspicion falling on him; indeed, he must have been the person who let the intruders inside in the first place!

Galfridas Hood took a step towards her, his sword raised. At the same moment another figure appeared in the doorway; Gwyneth gasped with relief when she recognized Ursus.

Another gasp came from behind her and she glanced back to see Marion le Fevre staring at the hermit, her face ashen with shock.

'It's all right,' Gwyneth explained rapidly. 'Ursus is a friend.'

'Gwyneth!' the hermit called, taking in the situation at a glance. 'Throw me the sword!'

At once Gwyneth tugged the bundle free. Galfridas Hood lunged towards her, but she let the sackcloth fall and held the naked sword in her hands. A tingle went through her, a thrill of certainty that whispered to her that she could do anything she chose, have all the power in England if she so desired. Was that what Hereward had felt?

Galfridas Hood stepped towards her again, cat-footed, his own weapon raised. Gwyneth watched him closely; he seemed still unaware that the sword she held was the Excalibur he craved for. Its blade was edged in glittering light and it seemed to sing out loud in the gloomy hut, promising that all she had to do was swing it and her enemy would be destroyed.

'Gwyneth!' Ursus cried out again.

The hermit's voice brought Gwyneth back to herself. Power like that was for warriors, for kings, not for the daughters of innkeepers. She threw the sword, and Ursus snatched it out of the air with a hiss like silk.

'A hermit.' The Hoodman's voice was sneering. 'A man of God. Put down the sword, fool, or I'll spit you like a chicken.'

It was true, Gwyneth thought despairingly. Excalibur or no, what could a man like Ursus know of swordplay, to defend himself against a man like Galfridas Hood?

The hermit retreated from the doorway,

treading softly backwards into the clearing. With a yell of fury the Hoodman sprang after him, and their swords clashed with a slice of gleaming iron. Gwyneth watched, one hand over her mouth, the other on the edge of the door frame. She had forgotten about finding Hereward, or her own escape; she was hardly aware of Marion le Fevre sobbing quietly behind her. All her attention was caught up in that small space where the blades were flashing.

After the first flurry of blows the two men backed off and circled warily around each other, sizing each other up. Galfridas Hood still looked confident, smiling. He raised his sword two-handed and slashed it down at Ursus; Gwyneth gasped, certain that the blade would strike off the hermit's head. But somehow Ursus was not where the blow fell; faster than thought he dodged to one side and struck the Hoodman's blade down as it passed him. Galfridas stumbled, caught off balance. Turning, he only just managed to parry as Ursus moved into the attack. The confidence in his face abruptly vanished, and joy welled up in Gwyneth as she realized that Ursus was at least his match in skill—and of course the sword he held could outfight any weapon cast by mortal hands.

'They'll kill each other!' Marion le Fevre whimpered. She had moved to join Gwyneth in the doorway, her hands clasped together and her face wet with tears. 'Oh, I can't bear to look!'

'Don't look, then.' Putting an arm round the embroideress, Gwyneth led her out of the hut and past the two battling swordsmen. Ursus was advancing now, forcing Galfridas Hood back into the undergrowth, where brambles threatened to trip him and drag him headlong. Every stroke Ursus made was clean and controlled; Excalibur obeyed him as if it were part of his body, the hermit's hand fitting the hilt so that it was impossible to see where man ended and sword began. Gwyneth struggled to tear her gaze away as she guided Marion around the edge of the clearing towards the path that would lead to the village and safety.

Before they reached it, they came to the place where Brother Timothy and Father Godfrey were trying to hold off the rest of the traitors. Gwyneth's heart, which had lifted when she saw how skilfully Ursus handled his sword, plummeted like a bird pierced by an arrow. The monk and the priest fought side by side, their backs against a huge oak tree. Brother Timothy looked exhausted, sweat pouring down his face. Father Godfrey had changed his sword to his left hand, while his right arm hung useless, the sleeve of his habit ripped in a jagged tear. The traitors pressed round them; in moments they would be overwhelmed, and then nothing would save Gwyneth and Marion from being recaptured. And Gwyneth had not even begun to look for Hereward.

She could do nothing except urge Mistress le Fevre through the bushes towards the path. Even though she admired the embroideress so much, she could not help becoming impatient at her weeping, or the way she stopped every few paces to disentangle her silken gown from the thorns that snagged it.

'Try to hurry,' she begged.

There was no response from Marion except for a renewal of her terrified sobbing.

Gwyneth was close to despair when more shouting came from ahead, away from the camp. A glorious flower of hope bloomed inside her as she saw Finn Thorson charge into the clearing, flourishing a drawn sword, and fall upon the traitors from behind. Half a dozen of the sheriff's men and a whole crowd of villagers followed him, yelling hoarsely as they surged across the camp.

Last of all, an exultant grin on his face, came Hereward.

Chapter Thirteen

Hereward skidded to a halt, astonished, when he saw his sister standing next to the weeping Marion le Fevre.

'You're safe!' Gwyneth exclaimed.

Hereward thought that was too obvious to need a reply. 'What's she doing here?' he demanded. He did not bother to hide his suspicions of the embroideress. Her servingman was the leader of the traitors, and now she herself was in their camp.

'She was a prisoner,' Gwyneth told him. 'I have to get her away.'

'Look after her, then,' said Hereward; there was no time to hear the whole of the story. 'I have to help Master Thorson.'

'Hereward, be careful!' Gwyneth shouted after him as he dashed forward into the centre of the camp.

Pausing to look round, he was startled to see Brother Timothy and Father Godfrey fighting side by side with a couple of Finn Thorson's men, beating off an attack from several of the traitors. Finn Thorson's huge figure was outlined against the fire in the middle of the clearing; as Hereward watched, his massive two-handed sword scythed round and cut down a traitor who came against him. At the other side of the clearing, among the bracken and thorns, Hereward was amazed to see Ursus battling with Galfridas Hood, and more amazed still as he watched the hermit's tireless, slicing sword-strokes, a display of skill that the Hoodman could not match.

More of the traitor's army were scrambling out of their tents, grabbing for weapons, to meet the unexpected onslaught from the villagers. Hereward spotted Clem Ludel fleeing from Dickon Carver who pursued him hard on his heels; the carpenter's scythe hissed as he slashed it through the air. Close by, Tom Smith brought his hammer down on the shoulder of one of the traitors, who collapsed to the ground and lay there moaning. To Hereward's relief he saw Hywel Smith advancing unscathed into the clearing with a puzzled expression on his face and a thick billet of wood in his hand; when Tom yelled at him, 'Fight, lad!' the puzzled expression cleared and he flung himself into the fray. Whether he understood the true purpose of his masters or not, the smith would fight loyally for his brother against all the enemies a king could have.

Hereward wondered wildly what he could do, regretting the loss of the hunting knife that Finn Thorson's man had taken from him in the woods. Grabbing a blazing branch from the fire, he jabbed it towards the face of a man who was bearing down on him, and the man veered off, yelling a curse. Then Hereward ran across the clearing to the nearest tent and held the flame close to the bottom of the hides until they began to blaze up. The flames cast a lurid red light over the shadowed clearing as they began to devour the nest of the traitors.

Hereward hurried on to the next tent, recognizing it as the one where Osbert Teller had kept him prisoner. As he approached, the dwarf stuck his head out of the opening, stared pop-eyed for a moment at the chaos in the clearing, and ducked back inside again.

Grinning to himself, Hereward set his burning branch not against the tent itself, but the ropes that held it up. The first rope snapped almost at once and the tent sagged to one side; a terrified yell came from Master Teller, and when Hereward burnt through another rope at the far side the whole of the tent collapsed. Still yelling, the dwarf thrashed about underneath it, struggling to free himself.

Hereward dropped the branch, grabbed a loose end of rope and pounced on top of the hide-clad figure, winding the rope around until the dwarf was trussed up like a chicken for the pot. His struggles gradually ceased, though the muffled curses that came from him continued for a long time.

Leaving him safely bound, Hereward glanced round to see what else he could do. More tents were blazing now, as well as a hut on the opposite side of the camp. Pale winter sun flooded the clearing, revealing the end of the attack. Most of the traitors were lying still, or standing under guard, their weapons thrown to the ground a safe distance away. Finn Thorson was calling his men to bring their prisoners to him, beginning to rope them together. Brother Timothy and Godfrey de Massard came to join him. Father Godfrey was gripping his right arm with his other hand; blood welled between his fingers, and as soon as they reached the sheriff, Brother Timothy made the priest sit down and began to examine the wound.

The rest of the villagers gathered round, knowing the fight had been won. Hereward jogged across the clearing towards them, only to pause when he saw Ursus appearing from the trees, a furious Galfridas Hood herded in front of him. He was astonished to see that the sword the hermit held at the Hoodman's back was his own, the exact one that he had found in the muddy lake-bed on John Brockfield's land. How had the hermit come to have it? Did Galfridas Hood know this was the sword he had questioned Hereward so closely about?

Ursus halted in front of Finn Thorson and thrust Master Hood at him. 'Here is the man you want,' he said, as calmly as if he were remarking on the weather. 'He is their leader, the Hoodman.'

'Is he indeed?' Finn Thorson's voice held a

vast satisfaction. He pulled a pair of iron fetters from his belt and clasped them round the Hoodman's wrists. 'It seems I've seen your face before. Aren't you Master Hood, servant to the lady who sews for the abbey?'

'Sews for the abbey!' Galfridas Hood spat out the words. 'That lady has other purposes in mind. Why don't you ask her?'

'I will.' The sheriff turned; following his gaze, Hereward saw Gwyneth approaching with Marion le Fevre, who still looked scared and tearful. 'Mistress le Fevre, what do you know of this man?'

The embroideress raised beseeching green eyes to the sheriff's face. 'Oh, Master Thorson, I beg your forgiveness!' she exclaimed. 'If I had known what manner of man he was, I would never have taken him into my service, or brought him to trouble the peace of your village.'

That was easily said, thought Hereward.

'She lies!' the Hoodman hissed. 'This was her plot all along. She is hand in glove with Henry of Truro. Who do you think told me about the sword?'

Marion le Fevre directed her green gaze at him.

Her face was full of sorrow. 'May God forgive you, Master Hood.' Turning back to the sheriff, her hands clasped pleadingly, she explained, 'I am a simple embroideress, Master Thorson. I stitched surcoats because these men told me they were a troop of mummers. I may have mentioned that Hereward had found a sword, but I thought it no more than a boy's play. What should I know of kings or traitors? Those are men's matters.'

'Don't be unkind to her, Master Thorson,' Gwyneth begged. 'She's telling the truth. The traitors were keeping her prisoner. Can't you see how frightened she is?'

The sheriff weighed up Mistress le Fevre for a moment in silence. 'What sword is this you speak of?' he asked eventually.

'That one,' Hereward replied, pointing to the shining blade that Ursus carried. 'I found it, and Master Hood wanted to know what I'd done with it. But I don't know why it's so important to him.'

Finn Thorson turned to Galfridas Hood, obviously meaning to question him further, but the Hoodman's mouth was clamped tight shut;

he would admit nothing more. Then his gaze returned to Marion le Fevre, who stared back at him beseechingly, her face streaked with tears.

Hereward still felt deeply suspicious, and he noticed that Father Godfrey was frowning at the embroideress, as if he too doubted her protestations of innocence.

Finally, Finn Thorson let out a long sigh. 'I cannot but believe you, mistress, when your life is dedicated to the sacred vestments of our abbey. Have a care, please, when you next appoint a servant.'

Marion le Fevre assured him fervently that she would, before dissolving into tears again and covering her face with her hands.

'Fool! Clodpole!' Galfridas Hood exclaimed. 'One day she'll take off her mask, and then you'll see I spoke the truth.'

'You won't be here to see it.' Matt Green spoke up from the crowd. 'It's the rope's end for you in Bristol.'

Galfridas Hood gave him a vicious glare, but said no more.

'There'll be a fair trial for all of you,' Finn Thorson promised, 'though I don't doubt what the end will be. Here,' he added to one of his men, 'rope him up with the rest. And some of you go to fetch the horses.'

As his men moved to obey, Hereward put a hand on the sheriff's arm. 'Master Thorson,' he said, 'Osbert Teller is here. I left him over there, tied up in a tent.'

Finn Thorson looked where he was pointing and saw the bundle that was Osbert Teller jerking and twitching as the dwarf renewed his efforts to free himself. The sheriff flung his head back and let out a bellow of laughter.

'Well done, lad,' he said, ordering one of his men to go and fetch this last prisoner. 'He was ever a troublemaker, though I doubt he'll hang for this—he's not enough of a threat to our king to warrant so harsh a punishment as that.'

As the men made ready to return to Glastonbury, Hereward felt a light touch on his arm. Ursus was standing beside him, still grasping the sword.

'That lady,' the hermit murmured, nodding towards Marion le Fevre. 'Who is she?'

'An embroideress,' Hereward answered, surprised at the hermit's interest. 'She's staying at the Crown while she works on vestments and altar cloths for the new abbey church.'

There was a slight frown between Ursus's brows and his blue eyes narrowed as he watched Mistress le Fevre being comforted by Gwyneth. 'Does she mean to stay long?'

'I expect so,' Hereward replied. 'The fabric she has would stretch from here to London, and she stitches at a snail's pace.'

'Indeed . . .' Ursus breathed out the word so softly that Hereward wondered if he was talking to himself.

'Would you like to meet her, sir?' he offered.

'What?' Ursus jumped as if his thoughts had been far away. 'No, Hereward, not now. The lady has too much on her mind to relish meeting me. Besides, I must go. My work here is done.'

'You captured the Hoodman!' Hereward's eyes lit up as he remembered how splendidly Ursus had fought. 'We owe you such a lot. Won't you come back to the village? Everyone will want to thank you.'

Ursus shook his head. 'I need no thanks. It was enough to have felt a sword in my hand once more, and to discover that I have not lost my old fighting skills.' There was a wistful note in his voice and he gazed into the distance as if he saw something there that Hereward could not.

Hereward suddenly wondered if Ursus had been a knight before he took up hermit's robes, and was remembering the splendid campaigns in which he had fought. It was not unknown for adventuring men to end their days in the solitude and simple life of hermits—and not for the first time Hereward sensed there were mysteries in Ursus's past that were beyond even Gwyneth's well-fed imagination.

Then, to Hereward's astonishment, Ursus laid the blade of the sword across his forearm and offered him the hilt. 'Will you take the sword again, Hereward—for the present?'

'But . . . it's not really mine,' Hereward admitted. He knew that although the sword had made him feel like the bravest knight, the hermit was a much more fitting bearer. 'Don't you want to keep it, since you liked using it so well?'

There was a longing in Ursus's eyes, a reluctance to give the sword up, that Hereward could easily understand, having held it himself for a few brief hours. Yet there was no hesitation in his voice as he agreed, 'It is indeed a noble sword, but the time is not right for me to take up arms again.' His gaze rested on the sword as he spoke, almost as if he was addressing it as well as Hereward.

With no other choice, Hereward grasped the hilt and felt once more the surging promise of power that the weapon held. 'Sir, what is this sword?' he whispered, sure that Ursus must have felt the same when he took it up.

Before the hermit could reply, Brother Timothy came up with Godfrey de Massard.

'Thank you for coming to look for me,' Hereward said, in greeting. 'Brother Timothy, where did you learn to fight like that?'

'Brother Peter taught me,' the young monk replied. 'He thought that I would need the skill, for the road that I must travel.' He glanced at Father Godfrey, and Hereward understood that he did not want to speak openly about his duties as a Protector monk. 'His fighting days were over,' Brother Timothy added, 'but he was a good teacher.'

Hereward realized that Father Godfrey was not paying much attention to what was being said. His face was white as the trampled snow, his black hair dishevelled and plastered to his forehead. He swayed, and Brother Timothy put out a hand to steady him.

'We must ride back to the abbey, Father,' he said, 'and you can show that wound to Brother Padraig.'

A brief look of irritation flitted across the priest's face, as if he was reluctant to admit to feeling pain or weakness, but he made no protest. Brother Timothy began to guide him towards the path, only to look back a moment later and say to Ursus, 'My lord, what will happen to the sword now?'

Ursus smiled. 'Do not fear, Brother. Hereward and I will take care of it.'

The monk bowed his head and moved off with Father Godfrey.

'What did he mean by that?' Hereward asked, his curiosity bubbling over like a pot left too long on the fire. 'Why did he call you "my lord"? And what do you want me to do with the sword?'

'Bring it tomorrow to the ferry, when the bell has rung for terce,' said Ursus. 'Let Gwyneth come with you as well. Then we shall do what has to be done.'

Nodding in farewell, he turned and walked off into the forest.

The fires were dying down in the clearing. Finn Thorson called out an order, and his men started to move off with their prisoners. Someone had found a mule for Mistress le Fevre to ride, with Hywel Smith at its head to hold its bridle.

As Hereward stood gazing at the sword in his hand, Gwyneth came hurrying towards him. 'Has Ursus gone?' she asked, sounding annoyed. 'He might have waited!'

'He wants us both to meet him at the ferry tomorrow, with the sword,' Hereward explained. 'Gwyneth, why is it so important?'

His sister's eyes flew wide. 'Of course, you don't know! Oh, Hereward, I'm sorry I was so horrible to you when you came to tell me about the traitors.'

'That's all right.' So much had happened since then that Hereward had almost forgotten their quarrel; it certainly didn't matter any more. 'You shouldn't have come looking for me here,' he added. 'You put yourself in danger.'

'It was my fault you went off by yourself,' Gwyneth said. 'Besides, you came looking for me.'

Hereward gave her a warm smile. It felt good to be friends with his sister again. Then alarm stabbed through him. 'What about mother and father!' he exclaimed. 'Are they angry with me?'

Gwyneth shook her head. 'I told them you went to help Master Short the basketmaker, and they assumed you were snowed up in his cottage last night. I suppose now they'll know what really happened, but with luck they'll be glad enough you're safe without wanting to know how you ended up in the traitors' camp.'

Hereward breathed a sigh of relief; any concern about what his parents might say about his adventure seemed small next to the battle that had just been fought and won, not just for the villagers of Glastonbury, but for King Richard himself.

Gwyneth took his arm and urged him to follow Master Thorson, so that they brought up the rear of the procession as it set off back to Glastonbury. Hereward could not help noticing that his sister cast a nervous glance at the sword as he thrust it through his belt and rested one hand on the hilt.

'There's something strange about this sword,' he remarked. 'Galfridas Hood was asking about it—and how did Ursus come to have it? Do you know?'

Gwyneth nodded, still looking uneasy. 'Hereward, about the sword. There's something I have to tell you . . .'

Chapter Fourteen

The bell for terce was ringing as Gwyneth and Hereward walked up the street past the abbey. Gwyneth pulled up the hood of her cloak against the cold, drizzling rain; the street underfoot was muddy with melting snow but at least the stones were less slippery than when they had been frozen over.

When they reached the corner of Tor Lane they met John Brockfield with a hazel switch in his hand, herding a gaggle of geese along the road.

'Good morrow!' he called. 'These are for your mother, for the Christmas feasting.'

'Thank you. Mother is expecting them,' Hereward replied, while Gwyneth pulled her skirt away from the outstretched neck of one inquis-itive goose.

Master Brockfield raised a hand in farewell

194

and went on down the street, his geese gobbling and pattering ahead of him. Gwyneth and Hereward hurried on, leaving the village behind and following the path through the woods until they came to the ferry.

Ursus was already there, standing beside the masterless boat. A sudden pang went through Gwyneth as she remembered how Bryan used to stand there, his bony figure poised over the water like a heron as he waited for passengers. He would never wait there again, and the village would need to find another ferryman.

'Have you brought the sword?' Ursus asked.

Hereward pulled back a fold of his cloak to show the sword stuck through his belt.

The hermit nodded approvingly. 'Come, then.' He climbed into the boat and took the pole, and when Gwyneth and Hereward were settled he pushed off.

The boat slid through the greenish-brown water; Gwyneth watched the smooth line of its wake with the strange feeling that she was crossing an invisible boundary into a land of marvels. What did Ursus mean to do to keep Excalibur safe, to keep England safe from evil men who would misuse the marvellous sword?

The boat nudged gently against the opposite bank and Ursus led the way along the path until they reached John Brockfield's pig shelter. Several of the pigs were rooting about in the muddy field, or wallowing in the pool at the centre of the old lake-bed, fat and pink with streaks of mud along their flanks.

Gwyneth began to understand why the hermit had brought them here. 'We have to put the sword back, don't we?' she said.

Ursus nodded. 'Hereward, this is for you to do,' he said, 'since it was you who found Excalibur after all these years. Cast the sword back into the water, and it will lie hidden there until the time is right for it to be revealed again.'

Reluctantly, Hereward drew the sword from his belt. His hand caressed the carved-dragon hilt, and he raised the blade to watch the play of light along its length.

Gwyneth saw the longing in his eyes and winced, remembering how the sword had filled her with the same sense of endless power. 'You can't keep it,' she whispered to him. The day before, she had explained to her brother how the sword he had discovered was Excalibur, the mystical blade of King Arthur himself, and how anyone who held it had the right to claim the throne of England. Hereward had been amazed, and Gwyneth thought she could see in him a mixture of sorrow and anger that the sword could never truly belong to him even though he had found it again after all this time. 'It isn't for you,' she said.

'I know.' Hereward let out a sigh. 'But it's hard to think of it down there, covered with mud. And it makes me feel . . .' His voice trailed off as he struggled to find a word.

'Powerful,' Gwyneth supplied. 'I only held it for a moment, but I felt it too.'

Hereward turned to her, something like relief in his eyes. 'Then it's not just me!' He shivered. 'Think how Galfridas Hood would have felt . . . he was crazed with power even without it.'

'That's why we have to throw it away,' said Gwyneth. More than anything she wanted Hereward to understand, to cast the sword into the water willingly so that he would be free of the longing for it. 'We both know, just a little, what it would feel like to be king—but can you

imagine it? King Hereward? Queen Gwyneth?'
She saw Hereward smile in spite of himself.
'Besides,' she added, 'England already has a true
king, even if he isn't here just now.'

Hereward nodded. Drawing himself up, he
turned to Ursus. 'I'm ready.'

The hermit smiled. He had listened to their
exchange in silence, and Gwyneth knew he
understood how important it was that Hereward
should make this decision for himself.

'Great power brings great responsibility,' he
said. 'Sometimes beyond the limits of this mortal
life. You have chosen wisely.'

Hereward raised Excalibur above his head. For
a moment a shaft of sunlight washed over it,
turning it to molten silver. Then he drew his arm
back and threw. The sword flew through the air,
turning over and over as it arced gracefully down
to earth, and with a last flash of steel disappeared
under the muddy waters of the pool.

'There.' Hereward let out a long sigh.

As the ripples died away, Gwyneth felt vaguely
disappointed. The moment should have been
more marvellous, though she hardly knew what
she had expected: perhaps a hand emerging from

the water, to grasp the sword and draw it down. Instead there was nothing but the grunting of Master Brockfield's pigs and the smallest tremor in the mud to show where the sword had landed.

'A deed well done,' said Ursus. 'Excalibur will sleep safe, until the time comes for it to return.'

'And when will that be?' Gwyneth asked. The sword—and England—were safe from traitors for now, with the Hoodman safely captured, but somewhere in the Welsh hills, Henry of Truro still plotted against their true king. If nothing else, the recent months had proved to Gwyneth, and her brother equally, that echoes from the past reached out time and again to cause ripples of unrest in the hearts and minds of modern men.

The hermit's blue eyes gazed into the distance, and Gwyneth felt as if he was a long, long way away from anything around them at that moment. 'When will Excalibur return?' he echoed, turning back to Gwyneth and giving her a warm smile— yet in his eyes there was something close to sadness. 'Ah, that is a question that not even the wisest man can answer. But rest assured, return it shall, as long as England needs her rightful king.'